I'm in LOVE with the VILLAINESS
She's so Cheeky for a Commoner

NOVEL

1

WRITTEN BY

Inori

ILLUSTRATED BY

Hanagata

Airship

Seven Seas Entertainment

HEIMIN NO KUSE NI NAMAIKINA! 1
© INORI. 2022

This edition originally published in Japan in 2022 by
AINAKA SHUPPAN, INC. Shizuoka.
English translation rights arranged with
AINAKA SHUPPAN, INC. Shizuoka.

Seven Seas press and purchase enquiries can be sent to
Marketing Manager Lianne Sentar at press@gomanga.com.
Information regarding the distribution and purchase of
digital editions is available from Digital Manager CK Russell
at digital@gomanga.com.

Seven Seas and the Seven Seas logo are trademarks of
Seven Seas Entertainment. All rights reserved.

Follow Seven Seas Entertainment online at
sevenseasentertainment.com.

TRANSLATION: Kevin Ishizaka
ADAPTATION: Nibedita Sen
COVER DESIGN: Nicky Lim
LOGO DESIGN: George Panella
INTERIOR LAYOUT & DESIGN: Clay Gardner
COPY EDITOR: Meg van Huygen
PROOFREADER: Jade Gardner
ASSISTANT EDITOR: Katy M. Kelly
LIGHT NOVEL EDITOR: E.M. Candon
PREPRESS TECHNICIAN: Melanie Ujimori, Jules Valera
PRODUCTION MANAGER: Lissa Pattillo
EDITOR-IN-CHIEF: Julie Davis
ASSOCIATE PUBLISHER: Adam Arnold
PUBLISHER: Jason DeAngelis

ISBN: 978-1-68579-697-6
Printed in Canada
First Printing: February 2023
10 9 8 7 6 5 4 3 2 1

Table of Contents

The Strange Commoner and Me

"To think a commoner would even fathom sitting next to me. Know your place!"

The commoner appeared dazed by my rebuke. She looked around herself, seemingly unable to comprehend her situation, then turned back to me. How dare she show *me* of all people such disrespect! It took all I had to rein in my fury.

My name is Claire François, and I was born to one of the Bauer Kingdom's most esteemed noble lineages. My father, Dole François, was entrusted with the kingdom's treasury as the Minister of Finance, making House François the third most powerful force in the country, second only to the royal family and the chancellor. We were elite even among nobility. It followed, then, that one such as myself didn't attend some ordinary school. No, I attended the Bauer Kingdom Royal Academy, a school that *solely* admitted the best of the best... At least, that was how it had been until the commoners wormed their way in.

"Ahh," the commoner before me said. "Claire?"

"Why I never! Who do you think you are, calling me by my first name?!" The likes of a commoner had no place addressing any noble in such a manner, much less a noble of my standing. My dear friends Pepi and Loretta glowered at the commoner in sympathy for my plight.

The commoner still seemed unable to grasp the situation. She met my eyes and said, "Miss Claire." Finally! That was proper for her station.

Goodness... The commoners thought they could act so imprudently merely because they attended the same school as we did. This was why they never amounted to anything; they simply didn't know their place.

"That's better," I said. "A commoner should show respect."

"Do you remember my name?" the commoner asked.

I never bothered to remember each and every commoners' name, but neither did I take kindly to having my memory challenged. Thus, I scoffed. If I remembered correctly, I had heard her name during roll call earlier: "Do you take me for a fool? You're Rae Taylor."

Right. She was Rae Taylor—the most accomplished of this year's transfer students, and an outsider who had been allowed to attend our illustrious academy despite her rank.

As I mentioned earlier, the Royal Academy was a school for the elite, one that had educated the nobility for generations. However, noble birth wasn't enough to earn a student the right to attend the academy. No, even the nobility had to pass rigorous tests and prove they were the cream of the crop to earn admittance. But for some reason, King l'Ausseil had allowed a small number of commoners to attend under the pretense of promoting "meritocracy." As if that weren't preposterous enough in itself, now one of those commoners was trying to sit next to *me*. As a high-standing noble lady, it was my duty to reestablish order in these halls.

I opened my mouth, ready to further admonish her, when instead—

"Yahoo!" she exclaimed with glee.

What a strange person this commoner was. Did she not understand that I was admonishing her?

"What's come over you? And to use such a vulgar expression... Goodness, what is the *matter* with you commoners?" The difference between commoners and my ilk was readily evident in our vocabularies alone. As things stood, these plebeians would ruin the academy's reputation. I muttered, "I respect His Majesty, but I cannot bring myself to agree with this policy at all."

"Me too, Miss Claire."

"Me three!"

My close friends Pepi and Loretta agreed with me, of course. The academy belonged to the nobility. It was no place for rabble.

If I could only do something about this particular commoner, the best of the transfer students, then the others would surely fall in line, no? With that goal in mind, I readied myself to speak—but before I could begin, the commoner called my name.

"Miss Claire?"

"What? It is most displeasing to see a commoner think she can simply call out to me," I curtly replied. Never could I have predicted her next words.

"I like you."

"Huh?"

What did she just say? My mind began to race. *"Like"? One can like many things: Foods, things, people—people? As in...? No, surely not—*

"Miss Claire, I love you."

"Wh...wh-wh-what...?!" What nonsense was coming out of this girl's mouth?! I'd come at her with all those harsh words and she was saying she *loved* me?! "What in the world are you saying?!"

"I'm saying I love you, that's all." The commoner looked at me with confusion, of all things.

I couldn't detect an ounce of ill will in her, but I couldn't take her words at face value either. What was she trying to pull? I thought for a moment, then stumbled upon a possibility.

"Hmph! The likes of a commoner trying to get on my good side? Don't waste your time." There was no end to the number of people who tried to curry my favor due to my family's standing. This commoner was doubtless just another one of them. I turned away with a huff.

"You're so cute."

"Wh...wh-what?!" I was accustomed to hearing my looks praised, but generally people called me things like "pretty" or "beautiful." I hadn't been called *cute* since, well, since I was a child!

Wait, no, that wasn't the problem here. The problem was that we were the same gender, yet the commoner was unmistakably showing...*interest* in me. "You... Are you trying to say you bat for *that* team?"

Women who fancied other women occasionally appeared in novels and plays, and they were often depicted as lecherous and debauched. Was this girl the same?

"Ah, I'm... Well, that doesn't matter. I mean, it's irrelevant to your cuteness—and, well, Miss Claire, you *are* cute."

"Eek?!" That settled it—she *was* the same as those foul perverts!

"Miss Claire, you hate me, right?"

"Of course!" There wasn't a single thing about this girl that I didn't hate!

"That's fine. Please keep teasing me. I love it."

"Wh-what in the world...?" I couldn't make sense of this girl, not in the least. She said she loved me, yet she didn't care if I hated her—and she furthermore *wanted* me to tease her. She was utterly incomprehensible. I stared at her as though she were some unknown life-form that had merely taken human shape.

"Now, let's get this super fun school life started, Miss Claire! We're going to have a great time!"

"What makes you think I'll have anything to do with you?!"

I hadn't the slightest inkling at the time, but this aggravating, cheeky commoner would go on to become the love of my life.

"What is *with* that commoner?"

"She's insane! How dare she speak that way to a noble such as yourself, Miss Claire."

I was joined by Pepi and Loretta for tea. We were at one of the many arbors located on academy grounds, which had been established to give students the perfect place to relax however they liked. This particular arbor was located at the center of the central courtyard.

Pepi was of House Barlier, a family that had a strong foothold in the financial world. She was a cute girl with milky skin and pink-tinged brown hair that came down to her shoulders. Loretta was of House Kugret, a family distinguished for its military officers. She was somewhat tomboyish and had short black hair. They were both close friends of mine, and we spent much of our time together.

The tea for our tea party had been imported from a country to the far west, and the many sweets laid out before us were from Broumet—one of the kingdom's finest restaurants. Of course, while the sweets were wonderful, nothing paired better with tea than small talk. Today, the topic of our chat was that strange commoner.

"Shouldn't we do something about her, Miss Claire? We can't let her off scot-free after everything she said to you."

"Yeah! She'll make a laughingstock of the academy at this rate!"

I understood very well where they were coming from. To deprecate me, one of the most prominent nobles, was to deprecate the entirety of the kingdom's nobility—such a thing could *not* be tolerated.

"Oh ho ho! Worry not, my friends." I gave them a strong, reassuring smile. "Driving a commoner or two out of the academy will be all too easy for me."

No matter how strange a person this commoner might be, she was still human. I could force her out of this academy simply by making it an unbearable place. It went against my nature to take advantage of a weak foe, but I was willing to stoop to such levels if it meant I could protect order in the academy.

"I knew you'd come through, Miss Claire!"

"So, what'll it be? How are you driving her out?"

"How indeed..." Even among aristocrats, bullying was known to occur. But as one of the most prestigious individuals of my social class, I had never considered committing such a deed myself, so I hadn't the faintest idea where to start. "Just for reference, what would you two do?"

Pepi answered first. "Me? Well...I suppose I'd try to sneak glass shards into her indoor shoes."

"G-glass shards?!" I exclaimed. *Did I hear her right? On the off chance the commoner didn't notice the glass and put on her shoes... How terrible! Oh, Pepi, you're only joking, right? You'd never do something so horrifying...right?* "I-I see... W-well, what would you do, Loretta?"

"Hmm... Why not light her uniform on fire?"

"Light her uniform on fire?!" I said incredulously. *Goodness gracious—the commoner might actually be hurt if we did that.*

Has bullying between nobles escalated to such a point without my knowing? Has the academy done nothing to maintain our school's moral backbone?

"But I'm sure Miss Claire wouldn't be satisfied with something as half-baked as *our* ideas."

"Yeah! I'm looking forward to seeing what you come up with, Miss Claire!"

Their enthusiasm was starting to scare me a little. Blindly going along with their suggestions would lead to simply horrific outcomes, so I needed to come up with something of my own. Something safer. "The two of you are still far too green," I said. "Such coarse violence doesn't even begin to qualify as bullying."

"Oh?"

"Do go on."

Their eyes shone with anticipation. Anticipation for what exactly, I didn't want to know. I felt like I was seeing a new side of my friends, one that I wished I could unsee. To be perfectly frank, they disturbed me quite a bit. I said, "I was thinking we could begin by pushing her from behind."

"You mean down the stairs?!"

"Or do you mean off the veranda?!"

Goodness. Calm down, you two. My opinion of you is plummeting rather drastically... I said, "Next, I was thinking I'd step on her."

"With high heels?!"

"On her face?!"

That would be dangerous! I could seriously hurt her if I stepped on her face with heels! I said, "Then I'd take her textbooks—"

"And cut them up?!"

"No, surely you'd have to burn them!"

Whyever would I ruin precious paper like that?! Are they unaware that all natural resources are a gift from God?! I said, "After that, I'd make sure she's alone and—"

"Imprison her?!"

"Miss Claire, you're a monster!"

The only monsters here are you two! My goodness. Have I somehow picked the wrong people to befriend? I said, "Next, I'll take some water and—"

"You'll deprive her of *water*?!"

"And then hold a tea party in front of her as she dies of thirst?!"

Who would hold such a barbaric tea party?! Honestly, are you even the same people you were yesterday? Weakly, I said, "Th-then I'd leave a flower vase on her desk—"

"And smash her face into it?!"

"Then grind her face into the shards?!"

How could I ever be so violent?! I don't care if she is *a commoner—one should never mar a lady's face!*

"Wow... I guess that's why you're top of the line, Miss Claire."

"Our ideas didn't even come close."

"I wonder about that..." I was a bit wary of my friends now. They were calm for the moment, but the strange enthusiasm they had displayed seconds prior reminded me a bit of that commoner. Perhaps something strange had been mixed into our tea and sweets? I'd heard some sweets contained liquor, but surely not these?

"A-anyway, you two can leave all the bullying to me. That commoner will be out of our academy before you know it." Having regained my composure, I lifted my teacup to my lips.

"No, please let us help!"

"Yes, please!"

"Absolutely not!" I said firmly.

"Miss Claire..."

"But why?"

"There's no need for you two to dirty your hands. My actions alone will be sufficient to drive that commoner out!" For as long as the commoner faced me, I wouldn't deign to borrow the help of others. My pride wouldn't allow it.

"Oh, but of course, Miss Claire..."

"We'd expect no less from you!"

My friends looked at me with deep admiration. They were apt to misunderstand things, so I was a little worried as to what thoughts might be running through their minds. "Listen carefully, you two. I don't need either of your help, all right? Am I clear?"

"Crystal!"

"Show us what you're capable of!"

And so my plan to bully that cheeky commoner moved forward. It wasn't until much later that I realized the plans I spent all that evening devising would only ever be considered a reward.

"Hello. It's been a while, Misha."

"Huh? Oh...Miss Claire. How do you do." Misha politely bowed her head.

I was unaccompanied by Pepi and Loretta; I had slipped away from them after spotting Misha, as I didn't want them to overhear what I had to discuss with her.

Misha Jur was a beautiful girl with silver hair and red eyes. We hadn't seen each other in quite a while, but her expression was as implacably indifferent as ever. Her cold eyes held no emotion as they regarded me.

"Congratulations on your admission to the Royal Academy. You may be a commoner now, but your family was once proud nobility. You're different from the rest of that lot. Please, feel free to drop the formalities with me," I said.

"Thank you, but I think it best if I refrain." Misha insisted we maintain our roles, something I thought was very like her indeed.

The head of House Jur had once held the rank of marquess. They had overseen matters involving land and architecture. I had heard they had been close with the royal family, so much so that the third prince, Yu, had visited their home to play when he was younger. Those of the Jur line were often stoic and earnest, and Misha had inherited those same traits—to the point that, at times, she was perhaps a little *too* diligent.

"Very well, then. I was saddened to hear of your family's misfortunes, however."

"It was unavoidable. Power struggles are the norm among the aristocracy, as is the loser's fall from grace." Misha didn't seem to be bluffing; she genuinely accepted the reality of her situation.

I detected neither trace of regret nor grudge within her. Misha's willingness to take defeat in stride was yet another trait archetypal of House Jur.

There were, more or less, four bastions of political power in the Bauer Kingdom. One was the royal family, naturally. They were the most powerful people in the country and had ruled for nearly two thousand years. History is never consistent, however, and things had started to change. The current royal family's power was tied more to their past influence than to anything concrete. Some noble families of the current era exceeded the royal family in terms of both financial holdings and political sway.

Another political bastion was House François, from which I hailed. We were the second greatest political power in the kingdom and had held the position of Minister of Finance for many generations. Both our finances and our political influence perpetually threatened to eclipse those of the royal family. Chancellor Salas Lilium did possess slightly more political clout than we did, but no one came close to rivaling the depths of our coffers. If any noble were ever so foolish as to offend my father, his grip on the kingdom's treasury could make their lives miserable... Although, of course, he'd never think to use his power to exercise such pettiness.

The third political bastion was Chancellor Salas Lilium's faction. I specified it as *his* faction and not House Lilium's because his house in itself held little sway to speak of. House Lilium was of fairly low standing; Salas had risen to the position of chancellor in a single generation purely by his own merit. While he had far less influence over the kingdom's finances, he had the ear of many other powerful people. It was an open secret among the nobility that it was only possible for the royal family to push its policies because of Salas's backing. His faction both revolved around and depended on his charismatic character.

The last political bastion was House Achard, whose family head held the rank of marquess. Their long history was second only to the royal family's, and their true standing was greater than their rank suggested. Several generations ago, the head of their family had lost a power struggle with House François, causing them to fall from the rank of duke—which I and my family enjoyed—to their current status. However, authority and pedigree carried immense weight to nobles, and in both regards, House Achard remained at the forefront. For now, they were the power most staunchly opposed to King l'Ausseil's meritocratic policies, and they represented the conservative faction that favored the tried-and-true system of peerage. House Achard didn't stand out particularly much in terms of present accomplishments, but they boasted a stable influence.

Forgive me—this explanation stretched a little long, didn't it? I say all this because Misha's house, House Jur, had lost a political battle against House Achard. House Jur had been a neutral party that refrained from siding with any of the aforementioned four powers, but they had earned the ill will of House Achard and been ruined all the same. Rumor had it that House Achard had been after House Jur's connection with the royal family, but the truth remained unclear.

"Do you have some business with me, Miss Claire?" Misha asked.

"Yes! Yes, I do!" I had almost forgotten. "It's about that room-mate of yours!"

"Rae? What about her?"

"Oh, I'll tell you what! That commoner is *insane*! She blathers the most absurd nonsense at every turn! Never have I met anyone so rude!"

"Huh? Oh, um... I'm most sorry to hear that." Despite being a little confused, Misha lowered her head and maintained her calm. "Just for reference, could you go into further detail as to what she said to you?"

"W-well..." I dithered. "She said she l-li...liked me..."

"I'm sorry? I couldn't quite hear you. Could you repeat that?"

"I-I said..."

"Yes?"

Why must I endure such embarrassment? One such as myself is far too proud to repeat such drivel! I muttered, "This is all that blasted commoner's fault...!"

"Er, Miss Claire?"

"Anyway, make sure that commoner learns to show the nobility proper respect!"

"But as far as I've ever seen, Rae is a fairly polite person..."

"In what way?! If one were to boil all the moisture out of rudeness until it consolidated into the shape of a person, she is what would be left!"

"Are we still talking about Rae?" Misha asked with a tilt of her head.

How strange. Did our impressions of that commoner really diverge? "Just out of curiosity, what manner of person do you consider that girl to be?"

"Hmm... I suppose I'd describe her as...normal?"

"*Normal?!* That—that *thing* is normal to you?!"

"Yes. I don't know what it is about her that rubs you the wrong way, but Rae really is just an ordinary girl who doesn't stand out much."

I was beginning to feel faint. *That commoner is* normal? *Oh dear, could it possibly be true that* all *commoners are like her and I've simply been none the wiser? I fear for Bauer's future, if so.*

"She's a bit on the quiet side," Misha continued, "and there's nothing particularly noteworthy about her. Oh, but she is a natural academic."

"Normal... That commoner is...*normal?*" I was still hung up on the "normal" part. What a frightful thing commoners must be. If this was the case, it truly would be for the best for nobles to lead the kingdom, lest the whole country come crashing down.

"How would you describe Rae, then?" Misha asked.

"She's a pervert."

"Huh?"

"I. Said. She's. A. Pervert! What is *with* her?! She tried to *court* me with *no* consideration to *either* her lowly status *or* the fact we're of the same gender! She can't *possibly* be sane!"

"I'm sorry, she tried to what? Court you?"

"Yes! I'm sure she only meant to tease me, but there's nothing funny about it! Not in the least!"

As I continued to vent, on and on, Misha tilted her head, confused.

"What is it?" I asked.

"Nothing. Well... I just can't help but feel you might have mistaken Rae for someone else."

"Impossible. She's that worryingly thin-looking commoner with black hair in a medium bob who's slightly taller than me, yes?"

"That's her. You remember her quite well."

"How could I not, after she left me with such a traumatic experience!"

"Is that right?" Misha began to chuckle.

"Excuse me? Misha? Is there something *funny* about all this?"

"Forgive me, Miss Claire. It's just that you seem to be enjoying yourself a bit."

"What?! Enjoying myself?"

"Yes," Misha said with a light smile. "As befits a noble, you always present a brilliant smile to everyone, but that's nothing more than a mask. You only show your real self to your friends— people like Pepi and Loretta. Am I right?"

"Of course n..." I began, but I trailed off. Perhaps she *was* right.

"Yet here you are, freely expressing your true feelings. I can't help but feel you're actually quite interested in Rae."

"You're wrong! You're *absolutely* wrong!" Was Misha insinuating that I was letting my guard down around that commoner? Impossible! "I just wanted to warn you, as her roommate, of her improper behavior—"

"Yes, I understand. I'll give her a stern warning. But have you considered the possibility that Rae only behaves that way toward you?"

"Huh?"

"As in, perhaps she finds you special?"

Wh-what? Special? I thought. "I-In any case, I believe I've made myself clear! I won't let her off the hook so lightly next time, so make sure her nonsense ends here!"

"I will, don't worry. I'll make sure to warn her nice and thoroughly."

"Please do! And with that, I bid you good day!"

I turned on my heel to leave Misha.

"Miss Claire, where did you go?"

"We were so worried when we couldn't find you."

"I'm sorry, Pepi, Loretta. I just had to take care of some business."

I met up with my two friends, and together we had tea at our usual arbor. The black tea my longtime maid Lene poured for me was delicious, but...

"She finds me...special?"

The words Misha had said stuck with me.

There was nothing pleasant about being liked by a commoner. Nothing at all...

Yet I just couldn't get that girl's blithe smile out of my head.

"Good day, Miss Claire!"

I was studying in the lecture hall before class when that commoner called out to me as though we were friends. Loretta saw my annoyed grimace and stepped in to block the commoner's way for me.

"Would you stop addressing us like we're friends? We live in a different world than you do. Isn't that right, Miss Claire?" Loretta said with a sneer. She wasn't one to pick on others, but she was certainly as much of a stickler for status and social rules as I.

"Ah... I don't have anything to say to you, minions. I'm speaking to Miss Claire. Good day, Miss Claire."

"Wha—you ingrate! Who do you think I am?" Loretta said. "I am of House Kugret, which has served the François family for generations!"

"So...Claire's minion, am I right?"

"M-Miss Claire..." Loretta, teary-eyed, turned to me for help. This rude commoner was perhaps too much for a sheltered noble lady such as herself to handle.

"Ugh, commoner..." I sighed. "Get over yourself. I have nothing to say to you. And don't you know 'good day' is used as a parting term?" Language usage within the kingdom had grown improper of late, even among aristocrats. The crass phrases the lower class used were becoming more and more commonplace, much to my dismay. Normally one such as myself wouldn't have deigned to correct the words of someone so inconsequential, but if I left this be, there was no telling what effect it might have on the academy as a whole. Hence, I had a duty to teach this commoner the proper way to speak in Bauer.

"So you say, but you still responded to me, and you even politely corrected my language. I just love that about you," she said.

There she went again with that "love" nonsense! "E-enough!" I exclaimed. "Are you trying to taunt me?"

"Yes!"

"You're not even going to deny it?!" She really was just making fun of me!

"Control yourself, Rae. And good morning, Miss Claire." Misha appeared then, grabbing the commoner's collar with the firmness of a cat picking up its kitten. I was relieved to see her. As sensible as she was, she would doubtless be able to rein in her roommate.

"Mishaaa, let go of me. I'm toying with Miss Claire right now."

"How can you be so shameless about it?!" I exclaimed. What was *with* her?!

"That's enough." Misha smacked the commoner on the head.

Give her a few more smacks for me, Misha, I thought. I then demanded, "Misha...control your kitten, would you?"

"Miss Claire, Rae is not my pet."

"But I would love to be *your* pet, Miss Claire."

"Oh, you be quiet!"

Goodness, we just kept going in circles whenever this girl was involved. How could she afford to be so silly all the time, and before a high-standing noble like myself at that?

"Miss Claire, you don't seem well. You should get some rest," the commoner said.

"And whose fault is that?! Just get out of here!" I snapped and shooed her away. She didn't seem to take the slightest bit of offense, however. How aggravating.

"A bit early to be so deep into your comedy routine, isn't it?" said a soft tenor voice.

"Master Yu..."

"Good morning, Claire. I haven't seen you fall apart like this in a long time." Yu chuckled.

This was Yu Bauer, the third prince of the kingdom. He had soft, curly blond hair and a gentle, cheerful smile—the quintessential image of a prince. He didn't let his good looks go to his head, however, and he was friendly with everyone, which perhaps factored into his popularity with the fairer sex.

I was a bit ashamed that he had seen me acting so disgracefully. I would have to clear up this misunderstanding. "Master Yu, this isn't what it looks like! I was just admonishing this commo—*ahem*, Rae here for acting with such disrespect."

"Is that so?" Yu turned his gaze to the commoner.

"I wasn't being disrespectful. Everything I said, I said out of love," she replied.

"What in the world are you talking about?!" I exclaimed.

"Aha ha ha!" Yu laughed.

The commoner was going so far as to prattle away in front of Yu. How dare she! A commoner talking to royalty in such a way was simply unthinkable.

I thought Yu might take offense, but he looked even more amused. "Rae Taylor, right? You were at the top of the incoming class if I recall correctly. I assumed you would be a bookworm, but you're actually pretty interesting." He flashed a gracious smile, which was wasted on the likes of her.

"Is that so? Thanks." Yet this commoner was wholly unaffected by that legendary smile, which had led many a lady to swoon. She even seemed to take issue.

"Rae, don't be rude now," Misha lightly scolded her. "Good morning, Master Yu."

"Oh, Misha. Good morning," Yu greeted her in turn. He was kind to everyone regardless of status, but he was particularly sweet to Misha, as the two were childhood friends. They had been close before her family fell to ruin, and it seemed that Misha had even nursed feelings for him when she was younger—not that she had a chance with him anymore.

"I apologize for Rae. I will make certain to chastise her later," Misha said to Yu.

"Don't worry about it. If anything, you could stand to speak to me less formally. We're all equals here at the academy, you know?"

"I will consider it..."

Their strange conversation seemed to hint that something lingered between them. That was when the commoner came over and whispered, "Miss Claire, what do you think? Have they rekindled their love?"

"Why is every thought that goes through your head so vulgar?" I sighed. Was Misha not her friend? How could this commoner be so unfazed seeing Misha long for such a hopelessly unrequitable love?

"What's up, everyone?" A lively, handsome, black-haired boy wandered over to greet us.

"Good morning, Master Rod," I said.

"Good morning, Brother," Yu echoed.

This boy was Rod Bauer, crown prince of the kingdom and Yu's older brother. He was first in line for the throne and the de facto next king.

"What're you guys talking about? Something interesting? Let me get in on this!" He let out a hearty laugh as he joined the conversation.

"There is absolutely nothing of interest here," I said. "Just one person trying to undermine the academy's morals!"

"Does that mean what I think it means?" the commoner said. "You want to undermine the academy's morals *with me*? Yes, please, let's do immoral things together, Miss Claire!"

"I will do no such thing!" I vehemently declared, not wanting to be misunderstood as being remotely associated with her. What nonsense was this commoner spewing before the king-to-be, anyway?

"The heck?" Taken aback, Rod looked at the commoner as if she were a rare animal.

"This is Rae Taylor," Yu said, chuckling. "She was at the top of the class of incoming students. She's pretty amusing."

Under normal circumstances, a commoner would introduce *themselves*, as was proper etiquette. Could this one not even manage that much?

"You certainly don't see her type among the aristocrats much. It seems my father's policy has given us all a good laugh," Rod said.

"Uh-huh..." the commoner said apathetically. Most people would have considered it an honor to even be addressed by Rod, but it seemed she didn't agree.

"A refreshing reaction. Rae, huh? I'll keep your name in mind."

"Do as you please."

"Rae, again, don't be rude," Misha chided.

"Do you know how many people would kill to be remembered by Master Rod?" I said. Even the ability to claim someone of the royal family knew your name could grant you an edge in high society. Was this commoner so ignorant that she didn't even know that?

"Yo, come join us, Thane," Rod called out.

"No thank you..." a sour voice replied.

My heart began to pound in its chest as I looked toward the back of the lecture hall. There sat the silver-haired boy for whom I secretly held feelings.

"I don't think Thane likes this sort of large group," Yu said with a troubled smile.

"Is there anything he *does* like?" Rod grumbled.

Thane was the kingdom's second prince. He had a cold beauty and a troubled air. It's true that he was the brooding sort, but that was exactly the thing that made my maidenly heart race. He was the polar opposite of that crass, loud commoner.

"Master Thane..." My heart leapt with joy as I said his name. My feelings were still unrequited; he likely only saw me as one of the countless nobles that populated his world. But that was fine for now. One day, fate would surely bring us together.

"Why don't you go talk to him, Miss Claire?" the commoner said.

I was so surprised that I thought my heart skipped a beat. Could this commoner have noticed my feelings? I stammered, "Wh-why should I?"

"Well, you like him, don't you?"

I was terribly shaken to have my crush announced publicly. I had been so sure my feelings would only ever come to light in a more romantic fashion—perhaps as Thane and I gazed into one another's eyes all alone on a moonlit beach—certainly not like *this*. In my surprise, I said something I didn't mean to. "O-of course not! I don't care for Master Thane at all!"

My voice echoed through the lecture hall. It was already too late.

Thane stood up and left the room, his face still expressionless.

"Oh... What do I do? I didn't mean to say that..." I said. *Oh no... What have I done? What if he comes to hate me for this? I can only hope he didn't misunderstand.*

"You should apologize to him later, Miss Claire."

"Why you—how dare a commoner like you act as though you know better!" I snapped. *This was all your fault in the first place!*

"Miss Claire," the commoner said with uncharacteristic seriousness. She held me with her strong gaze, making me flinch back.

"Wh-what?"

"Master Thane can be sensitive."

"Of course. You think I don't know that?" Thane was a soft-hearted individual. That was why someone like me needed to be by his side to support him.

"All the more reason you should apologize."

"E-enough out of you!" I stood up, slamming my chair back. I had made up my mind; I would do it. "I quite suddenly feel ill! I'll be leaving early!"

"M-Miss Claire!"

"Please leave me be!"

I left the lecture hall, not allowing Pepi and Loretta to follow. I had but one objective—to fix the misunderstanding between Thane and me.

"Master Thane! Please wait!"

I ran through the hall despite knowing such haste was improper. I managed to catch up to Thane right outside the academy entrance. He turned around and showed me his usual displeased countenance. Faced with such an expression, I found myself fumbling for words.

"What?" he said.

"Um, well, I..."

"If you have no business with me, I'm leaving."

Thane turned on his heel and made to depart. If I didn't fix our misunderstanding here and now, I feared he might never look my way again—and yet I couldn't find any of the right words to say. *Oh, if only I could be as frank with my feelings as that blasted commoner!*

For a moment, her stupid face came to mind.

I'M IN LOVE WITH THE VILLAINESS

"I like you."

"Master Thane, I like you!"

In disbelief, Thane stopped walking and spun around to look at me.

Oh dear. What have I done?

"Um, you see, uhh...what you heard earlier was all a, well, uh, a misunderstanding!" I was in too deep to back out now, so I mindlessly said the first thing that came to mind. *Wait, that makes me no better than that commoner!* I continued, "When I said I didn't care for you at all, I didn't mean it in the sense that I *hated* you."

Thane stared at me, silent.

I took that as a signal to continue. "Um...if anything...far from hating you, I..."

He continued to remain silent.

"I apologize...but I cannot finish that sentence just yet." At some point, tears had welled in my eyes. This was an unacceptable state for the daughter of House François. I hadn't spent all this time keeping up the act of a perfect noble only for it to come tumbling down now. *This is all that commoner's fault!*

"I see," he said finally. "I understand."

"Huh?"

"It would seem I didn't quite take your meaning. Forgive me." On Thane's face was a faint but unmistakable smile.

"N-not at all!"

Thane hesitated. "I'm sorry, but I don't think I know your name."

"I-It's Claire! Claire François!"

"Ah... Dole's daughter, then."

"That is correct!"

"Claire... You're very brave."

"Huh?" *What did he mean by that?*

"It must have been awfully embarrassing for a lady such as yourself to clear up this misunderstanding. And yet you still did."

"W-well...I couldn't very well allow it to stand."

"I see... Thank you, for showing consideration even to a man like me."

"But of course!" I gave the bow one offered royalty, which made Thane smile again.

"You're a good woman, Claire. You'd be wasted on someone like me." As Thane said that, he neared.

Huh? Huh?! I grew increasingly flustered as he drew closer and closer. Thane stopped right before me and looked into my eyes. I couldn't help but blush like a tomato.

Then he said something too faint for me to hear.

"U-um...?"

"Let's go back," he said again, louder, as he gave me a pat on the shoulder and then walked back into the academy.

I followed after him, my heart racing a mile a minute.

I had worried over how things would go, but it had been fine—a little romantic, even. I was too worked up to think through what I had said.

But all's well that ends well, I guess. Hmph. I suppose I could afford that commoner some gratitude.

"You sure are cheeky for a commoner!"

"Yes! Cheeky, that's what I am! Please berate me more!"

The commoner had come pestering me first thing in the morning yet again. It had already been a week since the day of the entrance ceremony, yet our little routine continued. Pepi and Loretta had long since abandoned any hope of deterring her, instead choosing to ignore her presence. I'd have liked to do the same, but when I'd last tried to ignore her, she'd said, "Oh, do you give up, Miss Claire? Then I suppose that means I've won and can do whatever I like now. First, I think I'll have myself a fiery, passionate ki—"

You get the idea. Ignoring her only made her more of an annoyance, so I had no choice but to entertain her antics somewhat.

Of course, that didn't mean I was content with always being run around in circles. That day, I intended to show her who was really in charge. I said, "I won't be made a fool of any longer."

"Oh?"

I put on a daring smile. "You are aware we have tests tomorrow, are you not?"

"Of course."

Tests at the academy could largely be divided into three categories: culture, etiquette, and magic. We would be assessed on all three subjects tomorrow, then ranked by individual subject and overall score.

"We'll have our test scores decide things once and for all. If I win, you will leave the school." It was a brilliant idea if I said so myself. By besting her in these coming tests, I would break her spirit and at last bring a stop to her rampage.

But she shot me down with an instant rejection. "What? No way, I don't want to."

"At least consider it!" I snapped back, stomping my feet in frustration. I taunted, "Or do you mean to tell me the top-scoring transfer student is a coward?"

"But if I leave the academy, I won't be able to toy with you."

"Again, how can you be so shameless?!"

"Ha ha ha. You're so silly."

"*I'm* the one who's silly?! Me?!" To tell the truth, I kind of did feel I acted absurd when I was around her, much to my chagrin. "Enough already! Just accept my challenge!"

"Hmm... All right, how about this? If you can't beat me, then you must grant me a favor."

"Huh? Why in the world would I agree to that?"

"Hmm? Are *you* the coward, then? I thought you were at the top of the class of continuing students."

Blood rushed to my head. *Oh, so that's how it's going to be?*

I'd attended the Royal Academy since kindergarten and had consistently achieved some of the highest marks, only bested by the three princes. I couldn't possibly lose to a commoner, not in a million years. "Are you trying to taunt me? Very well, then. I accept your terms."

"Heh heh. Thank you."

"What do you imagine you're thanking me for? You may as well pack your bags now."

"Thank you for the encouragement!"

"I most certainly am not—ugh! Misha!"

"What is it?" Misha approached from where she had been watching from the sidelines.

"Will you be our witness? If I achieve the higher score on this test, this commoner will leave the academy. If, for some reason, I can't beat her, I will grant her a single favor."

"Expulsion and enrollment within the institute are decided by the king. Such a condition can't be enforced."

"There will be no need to enforce it. The commoner will leave the school of her own volition, shamed by her lack of talent."

"Are you really okay with this, Rae?"

"Yep."

"Then it's decided. We can't have her going back on her promise, so you will be the witness, Misha. That's fine with you, isn't it, commoner?"

"Yes! I'm getting excited just thinking about what I might order you to do for me!"

"That's *if* I lose, which will never happen! Now, swear to God!"

"I swear to God!"

"I am witness to your accord."

In this country, a vow sworn to God carried heavy significance. Breaking such a vow would lead an individual, noble *or* commoner, to be scorned by all. The stakes were especially high with nobles, however, as one's good family name was on the line.

But of course, I wouldn't have proposed such a challenge if I weren't certain of my victory.

I was in perfect condition the next day. Our first test was on culture. It mainly covered Bauer's history, customs, and literature. The literacy rate among commoners was only around 40 percent, so it made sense then that nobility—and by extension, I—had an overwhelming advantage in this subject. I would most definitely score higher on this test and consequently would already have a higher overall score as well.

"Hee hee, go ahead and struggle as much as you like, commoner." I was overflowing with confidence as I composed a traditional poem for the test.

Our next test was on etiquette, which covered just that— etiquette. We dined together for the event and were graded by proctors on our manners.

The test posed no challenge to me whatsoever. Dining etiquette had been drilled into me from early youth, and formal dining was something I engaged in daily regardless. I ate as I always did for the test, letting muscle memory handle things and only paying slightly more attention than I might usually.

I took a glance to see how the commoner was doing only to find her staring at me with an awed expression. *Wh-what is she doing...?*

That was two of three tests out of the way. Naturally, I was also favored in etiquette as a noble, so there was no way the commoner could hope to best me there.

Our last test was on magic. If the commoner were to beat me in any category at all, it would have to be that one.

King l'Ausseil's shift toward meritocratic policies could perhaps have been better described as a shift toward policies that favored those of magical skill. Magic was a potent resource, so it was no wonder King l'Ausseil wanted to prioritize it. Unfortunately, many nobles opposed the change.

The strength of one's magic was both somewhat inborn and somewhat acquired, but there generally wasn't much difference in arcane strength between the nobility and commoners. Because of that, a commoner could easily be ranked superior to a noble despite a lack of prestige or pedigree. I had to wonder, could magic not become the very undoing of our kingdom's social order?

Our magic test was held outside. We were assessed on basic aptitude as well as our ability to wield magic tools.

Some of the noble students became dejected upon finding out they had low aptitude for magic. Of course, arcane skill wasn't the only means by which noble merit could be judged, but everyone wanted powerful magic regardless. Lofty ambitions simply came with the territory.

As for how I did—

"You're amazing, Miss Claire!"

"I can't believe you got high aptitude in fire!"

"Oh ho ho ho! 'Tis only natural for me!"

Only natural for me, indeed. I was gifted even when it came to magic. High aptitude was essentially as good as super aptitude at a discount, as only a vanishingly small number of people in the world were blessed with the latter. Moreover, my magic was of the fire attribute, the best one for offensive magic. That commoner had probably hoped to overcome me on this test, but it seemed her luck had run dry.

"I'll leave that commoner speechless this time for sure!"

Later that night, for some inexplicable reason, the commoner visited me in my room, positively radiating cheer.

"And so I'm here to reenergize!"

"Please leave."

I drove her away, of course.

The time had come for the test results to be posted, three days after the fact.

"Do you know you have dark circles under your eyes?" I spotted the commoner waiting before the notice board out in the hall after classes and called out to her. Ordinarily, I never would have bothered to go out of my way to speak to *any* commoner, but I couldn't help but tease her upon seeing those bruises under her eyes. A little taste of her own medicine.

"Ah. That's because I couldn't sleep a wink last night..."

"Oh ho ho ho. How very unfortunate. But a promise is a promise now, isn't it?" I was sure today would be the commoner's last day at this academy.

"What's that? Oh, these bruises aren't because I was worried.

I just couldn't stop daydreaming about what favor I should ask of you, and before I knew it, it was morning."

"That's what you meant?!" I exclaimed with some exasperation. "You *genuinely* think you can beat me...? Well, you're optimistic, I'll give you that." I covered my mouth with my hand and let out a shrill mocking laugh.

"There's no telling who'll win until we see the results."

"Oh, I'd say it's perfectly obvious." I glared at the commoner, not liking to see her so...unfrazzled.

"Heh heh. You two certainly have become close," Yu said as he arrived. He had on his usual soft smile as he turned to the commoner. "Feeling confident, Rae?"

"A bit."

"Ha ha, good luck. How do you think you did, Misha?"

"I can at least say I tried my best." Misha didn't seem all too pleased to be addressed by Yu, understandably. While I was hesitant to stoop to the commoner's level and speculate on other's affairs, it did seem to me that Misha had some unresolved feelings for Yu. But there was nothing to be done about their difference in status. Her love would never bear fruit, and she knew it—hence why she was so reserved in his presence.

"All right, then, let's see who's coming in second." Rod appeared as well, brimming with confidence and rightfully so. He had talent worthy of a man who would be king. His confidence was nothing like the commoner's empty bravado.

We stood at the front of the crowd, right before the notice board. I looked behind me and saw Thane, who seemed more disgruntled than usual. He was by no means an incapable individual—far from it. He was much more gifted than the average person could ever hope to be. The problem was that he compared himself to Rod and Yu, an unparalleled prodigy and a genius, respectively. It didn't matter how much talent he himself possessed, he felt unworthy compared to his brothers.

"It's here." Misha's voice brought me back to reality. An office staffer was approaching with a sheet of paper.

"Are you ready to taste defeat?" I asked smugly.

"No, but I'm ready to enjoy my request."

Talk big while you still can, I thought as I looked at the culture test results being posted.

I was then rendered speechless.

CULTURE TEST RESULTS

1st	Rod Bauer	(100 pts)
2nd	Yu Bauer	(98 pts)
2nd	Rae Taylor	(98 pts)
4th	Claire François	(95 pts)
...		
...		
7th	Misha Jur	(90 pts)
...		
...		
10th	Thane Bauer	(87 pts)
...		
...		

"What?!" *The commoner took second?! She's* above *me?!*

"Not bad! I expected me and Yu to finish first and second, of course, but way to go, Rae!" Rod said.

"Nice one, Rae," Yu said.

"Thank you very much." The commoner gave me a proud look.

I was humiliated. *I...lost? I, a lady of the most powerful noble house, scored lower on the culture test than a* commoner...? I clenched my fists until my knuckles turned white and trembled ever so slightly.

But the truth remained.

"M-Miss Claire, pull yourself together!"

"Don't worry! This has to be some kind of mistake!"

"O-of course..."

Pepi and Loretta consoled me, but I couldn't recover my calm. While I was still shaken, the results of the etiquette test were posted.

ETIQUETTE TEST RESULTS		
1st	Yu Bauer	(100 pts)
2nd	Rod Bauer	(98 pts)
3rd	Claire François	(97 pts)
4th	Thane Bauer	(95 pts)
...		
...		
8th	Misha Jur	(90 pts)
...		
...		
22nd	Rae Taylor	(75 pts)
...		
...		

Life flowed back into me. "*Weeeell*, would you look at that!"

"Congratulations, Miss Claire!"

"I knew you could do it!"

"Thank you, my friends." I managed a proper response to Pepi and Loretta this time. The commoner's earlier score on the culture test had to have been a mistake, or perhaps a fluke, just as Loretta said. Surely.

"Your earlier score was sheer luck. The wolf has been stripped of her sheepskin," I gloated.

"Indeed," the commoner flatly agreed.

Hmph. Bluff all you like. I know you're torn up on the inside.

Finally, the results of our magic test went up.

MAGIC POWER TEST RESULTS		
1st	Rae Taylor	(Immeasurable)
2nd	Misha Jur	(98 pts)
...		
...		
6th	Claire François	(92 pts)
...		
8th	Thane Bauer	(90 pts)
9th	Rod Bauer	(88 pts)
9th	Yu Bauer	(88 pts)

"What...?" I was rendered speechless yet again. Immeasurable? Was such a thing even possible? "Commoner! What is the meaning of this?!"

"Hmm, good question!" the commoner said with a big grin.

Why you little...!

Our overall scores were posted at the end.

COMPREHENSIVE RESULTS

1st	Rod Bauer	(286 pts)
1st	Yu Bauer	(286 pts)
3rd	Claire François	(284 pts)
...		
...		
8th	Misha Jur	(278 pts)
...		
...		
10th	Thane Bauer	(272 pts)
...		
...		

*Note, due to the unprecedented results attained by Rae Taylor, her score will be handled separately at this point in time. The Academy will review its methods of evaluation going forward.

"That can't be..." I had taken these tests with utter confidence in my victory, but this result was far from what I had expected. The commoner possessed power beyond what the test had been designed to measure. Just who was she...?

"But you placed right after the two princes! That's amazing!"

"That's right! We knew you could do it, Miss Claire!"

"Yes... Yes, that's right." Pepi and Loretta had a point. I might not have achieved an overwhelming victory like I had planned, but I hadn't lost either. I could accept this. I let myself breathe a sigh of relief when—

"Misssss Claaaaaire!"

"Eeep!"

The commoner came over, all smiles. "What's wrong? You look like you just saw a ghost."

"I do *not*. What do you want? As you can see, our competition has been voided."

"What do you mean? You were unable to beat me, Miss Claire."

"Huh?" I hadn't a clue what the commoner was getting at.

"Don't you remember our deal? If you beat me, I would leave the academy. If you didn't beat me, you would grant me a favor."

"Don't patronize me; I remember, but our match failed to meet its conclusion."

"Right. In other words, you didn't beat me."

"Oh..." The agreement was that I'd do one thing she said *if I didn't beat her*. That included any case in which there was no clear winner, as now. "H-how cowardly!"

"Yep, I left the wording ambiguous to trick you!"

"Then it doesn't count!"

"What? You'd break your vow? But you swore to God."

"Ngh..."

The commoner had clearly tricked me, but I *had* sworn. I couldn't double back on my vow. I had much more at stake than she did.

"Fine, then... Name your request..."

"I knew you would come through, Miss Claire! I love you!"

"That's enough. Just hurry up and tell me!"

Knowing her, she would definitely demand I do something outrageous. I braced myself as best I could, when, to my surprise, she smiled softly and said, "I ask that you never give up."

"Huh?"

"No matter how hard things get, don't give up until the very end."

Flummoxed, I stared at her. "Is that all?"

"Yes."

"Huh... I thought you would ask me for something completely unreasonable."

"Would you prefer that?"

"No, this is fine, thank you very much!" I said quickly. I feared she might change her request if I allowed her the opportunity. "I swear to God that I will not give up. I promise never to abandon hope and to keep going until the end."

"That's wondrous, Miss Claire," she said with some applause.

"I won't lose next time." I wouldn't allow myself to be disgraced twice. With renewed will, I turned to leave.

"Oh, Miss Claire?"

"What is it now?"

"I love you."

"Well, I hate you!"

Goodness gracious. Just what was with this girl? At any rate, I realized that from this day forward, I would have to change my evaluation of her the slightest bit.

"Hmm..."

I was having a lazy morning stuck in bed. I knew I would have to get up soon and start freshening up, but I was simply too preoccupied with my thoughts.

The academy allowed students to bring up to two servants with them. Most of the commoner students couldn't afford such a luxury, but I was the daughter of House François; it was only natural I'd have gifted servants to attend to my needs.

"Good morning, Miss Claire."

"Morning, Lene."

"Is something the matter? You're making quite the face."

My servant, Lene, approached. She had flaxen hair, hazel eyes, and was always composed. Seeing that I wasn't getting out of bed, she shrugged and began picking out clothes from my dresser.

"Miss Claire, one of your buttons is undone."

"What does it matter? It's not like anyone's around to see."

"Of course it matters. Loose manners lead to loose morals."

"Fine." I reluctantly fastened the top button of my pajamas.

"Is something on your mind?"

"Well...yes. There's a certain someone that's been causing me grief of late."

I was back at the François family home for the weekend. Normally, I spent weekends at the academy dorm, but I had some special business to take care of this time around.

"That Rae girl, I'm guessing?" she asked.

"Who else could it be? I can't believe she's actually coming to take the interview to become my maid..."

Today was the day we were interviewing for the position of the second servant I'd be bringing to the academy. I doubted there were many who could measure up to Lene's level, but if this would-be servant of mine were to serve me publicly at the academy, they needed to at least be somewhat gifted so I wouldn't lose face.

Of course hiring that commoner was simply out of the question.

"Hee hee. So there's someone even you can't handle."

"Please. One would need to be out of their mind to tolerate her. I'm far too delicate a lady to put up with such a character."

"Oh, I'm sure. That girl is far too much for a lady such as yourself." Lene didn't stop dressing me as we chattered. There were no pauses in her movements, proof of her years of experience serving me.

"Which brooch would you like to wear today?" she asked, gesturing to my jewelry stand.

"I'll let you pick this time."

"In that case... Since this interview will be formal, something fittingly refined would do well. How about this one?" She pointed to a silver brooch with a jet-black gemstone carved in the shape of a flower and adorned with pearls. It was the perfect choice.

"That'll do."

"Let me put it on for you, then."

Lene was the prime example of how a maid should be: perfectly in-tune with their master. I had nothing but appreciation for her ability.

"Your application is rejected."

"Please, isn't there any way?"

"No! Now get out!"

The source of my grief wouldn't back down without a fight. To my ire, she had *actually* applied for the position of maid, and somehow even made it to the final interview. Unbelievable!

"Miss Claire, are you sure we can't hire her? She has such exceptional skills..." said the chief maid, who had handled the screening process.

Despite being a commoner, Rae had a decent education and was somewhat well versed in etiquette. Her magic aptitude was also high, so she could double as protection. In short, while I hated to admit it, she was a splendid candidate if we went by ability alone. But of course...

"The problem is her personality! I would never have a moment's rest if I had to be around a maid like this all day."

"But it seems she's very loyal."

"It's not just loyalty, madam. I am in love."

"And I simply can't have a maid who talks to me like that!" I squawked. *Somebody, please...bring me Lene so she can soothe me.*

A man walked in at that point. "What's this racket?"

"Master..."

"Father..."

He looked impeccable in a high-quality suit and held an ivory and rosewood cane. He looked at me, then cast his sharp gaze toward the commoner. The commoner didn't so much as fidget, even though Father's gaze could make even the slyest of nobles squirm. Was the commoner brave or just too dense to care?

The chief maid said, "We are hiring a maid to accompany Miss Claire at the academy, but the lady disagrees with my selection."

"I see. Well, our chief maid would select only the finest candidate. What is the issue, Claire?"

"Her personality is impossible. She's always attempting to make a fool of me."

"Aha... So the issue isn't a lack of qualifications but a lack of respect for her employer. Shouldn't that disqualify her?" he said to the chief maid.

"I wouldn't say that's the case. She applied for the position because she wants to serve Lady Claire. Unlike most interviewees, she seems to have no financial motivation."

"Well, she might just be saying that."

"When I asked her how she would serve the lady if she were hired as a maid, her answer was exceedingly well thought out and specific. I believe her to be genuine."

My father thought for a moment. "But Claire is unfond of her, and it is her decision in the end."

"That...is true."

"Thank you, Father!" I said. *Now I won't have to put up with having this commoner always by my side!*

"Your Grace, please allow me to be so impudent as to speak to you directly."

Just as I was celebrating, the commoner directly addressed my father. Naturally, he furrowed his brows.

"You, a commoner, dare request to speak to a noble? And to the Minister of Finance, no less? It seems Claire was correct in her judgment. One can only tolerate so much impudence."

"Irvine Manuel."

My father's expression lost all warmth. A mocking sneer still remained on his face, but his eyes were not smiling. "And who might that be?"

"March 3rd, five hundred thousand gold."

I hadn't a clue what was going on, but my father was oddly silent. "Father?"

"Claire, chief maid, please leave us."

"I cannot allow that! At least let me call for a guard—"

"That is an order," he said with a tone of finality.

The chief maid had no choice but to back down.

"Must I leave too?" I asked.

"I'm sorry, Claire. I just want to confirm a few things. Please understand," he said gently.

"Very well..." Together with the chief maid, I left the room.

Around thirty minutes or so passed before my father allowed us back in and said: "You will hire this person as Claire's maid."

"Why?!"

"She is trustworthy. She will be suitable for the role."

"I don't accept this! What did you say to my father?!" I asked the commoner.

"Nothing special. I just told him about my love for you."

"Would you stop joking around?!"

What is the meaning of this? Just what could this commoner have said to win Father over? She didn't entice him with her body, did she? No, Father would never be swayed by such a thing. Then what?

"Father, do you genuinely mean for someone who speaks to me like this to attend me?!"

"Having spoken to her, I am convinced of her earnestness. She is completely loyal to you, Claire."

"But she's loyal for the wrong reasons! She simply wants to make a fool of me!"

"Claire," he said a little sternly. I didn't have a say in the matter, it seemed. "It's easy to find someone obedient to serve at your side. But I want you, as the only child of the François family, to show me you have what it takes to rein in a servant."

"Mgh..." While I would never hold government office, as the future wife of someone who would, I'd be served by many servants one day. For that reason, I had to prove to my father that I could handle this commoner. "Do you truly insist we hire this commoner?"

"I do."

"Very well, then." I had to admit there was logic in his words. Plus, as a noble, it would be unbecoming of me to argue on a purely emotional basis. I took a deep breath and faced the commoner head-on. "As my maid, you must do as I say! Don't think I'll go easy on you!"

"Thank you very much! I will do my best!"

And so, the commoner artfully wormed her way into my employ. But just what could she have told Father?

Dole François

AFTER MAKING CLAIRE and the chief maid leave the room, I looked back at the young girl before me. She appeared a bit tense but otherwise displayed no hint of fear, despite my presence. A brave one, then.

She knew of my connection to the revolutionary forces. Moments ago, she had named the treasurer, the date I last sent funds, and the exact amount of those funds. I had been careful, sparing no effort to amass a number of proxies so nothing could be traced back to me, but it seemed there had been a leak. The girl looked to be about the same age as Claire, but she was clearly no ordinary child. While I felt some sympathy, I could not let her leave my home alive.

"Now, then. Who are you, and what do you know?" I said.

Killing her would be all too easy, but first I had to gain what information I could. The revolution I desired was still a ways off; if there was a leak at this early stage, then I needed to make some major course corrections.

"Your Grace, allow me to say first that I'm not your enemy."

"Hmph. Then what are you?"

"Your ally. Allow me to help you carry out your grand plan," she said, then bowed her head.

"What is your name?"

"Rae Taylor."

"A commoner?"

"A commoner."

"And what's this about becoming Claire's maid?"

"Ah, that. Just something I'd *like* to do. My real goal is to save Claire."

I quickly concealed my surprise. How did she know that Claire might require saving? I hadn't shared the full scope of my plan with anyone, not even Arla and Irvine. "Allow me to ask you something."

"Anything."

"How much do you know of what I'm attempting to do? Tell me all you know."

"Gladly."

Rae went on to tell me what she knew without hiding a single thing. She told me of how I was trying to do away with the corrupt aristocracy, of how I was secretly funding the revolutionary forces, of how I was trying to induce a revolution in the kingdom that would end in the death of the corrupt nobles, and of how I was dragging my own daughter into this mess. "I have nothing but respect for what Your Grace is attempting, but I cannot allow Miss Claire to die. I wish to save her."

"How do you know all this?"

"You wouldn't believe me if I told you."

"I'll decide whether I believe you or not. Tell me."

"Very well, then," she said with some reluctance. What Rae proceeded to tell me was certainly hard to believe. She claimed to be from another world, one in which the world I knew was the setting for some story with which she was intimately familiar. It was an absurd claim. But she *did* know everything about my plan, and she even told me of an incident to come—Mt. Sassal was soon to erupt and plunge Bauer into chaos. She went a step further and suggested we make use of the eruption.

If this was all a bluff, she was one hell of an actress.

Having been exposed, I had no reason to pretend to be the arrogant noble I wasn't and so changed my tone.

"Do you believe me?" she asked.

"You leave me no choice," I said. "But what do you wish to do with Claire?"

"It may be hard for you to understand, with your values, but I love her."

"Pardon?"

"Of course, I understand the difference in status between us and know we have no hope of ever being wed. But I at least want to serve her as best as I can for as long as I can."

"Hmm..."

"I know you believe you have no choice but to bring Claire down with you, but I can change that." A gleam of sincerity shone in Rae's eyes. Indeed, I could not grasp the thought of love between two members of the same sex, but I understood that this girl genuinely cared for Claire. She wasn't lying.

Then again, I supposed it didn't really matter. Her love could be a lie, and that would be fine—so long as Claire was saved. I would have sold my soul to the devil if it meant my daughter could be spared. I'd have searched for a way for her to survive myself if I could, but even if I had found one, what way of life could Claire lead other than that of a noble? I had no doubt she'd sooner choose to take her own life than to prolong one defined by disgrace.

"And how would you change her fate?" I asked.

"I'll make her stand against the nobles."

"Oh...?"

"It'll require her to oppose you, at least outwardly, if that's all right with Your Grace."

Rae's plan was as follows: The eruption of Mt. Sassal would bring about many casualties. In the name of restoration, I would hike taxes and earn the antipathy of the citizens. Claire would then object to my actions with Rae's encouragement.

"I doubt things will go as perfectly as you plan," I said.

"Me neither. But I'll make it work anyway."

"And becoming Claire's maid serves this purpose?"

"It does. She still doesn't harbor any doubts about what it means for her to be a noble, nor does she recognize the problems in this kingdom. I'll change that. Ultimately, I plan for Miss Claire to be seen as one of the proponents leading the revolution. She'll lose her noble status, but at least she'll be alive."

"Hm..." Rae's plan was one I had considered myself, but it would have been impossible to carry out without a collaborator to change Claire's mind in the first place. I needed someone to whom I could entrust Claire and in whom I could confide my grievances with the kingdom, but such a convenient person had not, until this point, existed. Now here was Rae, telling me she could be the one to make that plan work, to make Claire face our kingdom's shortcomings and help her grow as a person. I hadn't even given much thought to the notion of letting Claire grow. For that, I was a failure of a father.

"I understand," I said. I decided to believe Rae for now. She was capable, and she had more use as a pawn than killed for caution's sake. "I'll allow you to become Claire's maid."

"Thank you very much."

"Send me periodic reports by letter so we can align our plans."

"I will."

"I take it you're fine with keeping all this from Claire?"

"Of course. If she knew, she would oppose it. We'll tell her everything once things are far enough along that there's no risk."

"Hmm..." Rae knew Claire's personality well. However... "Very well. Starting today, we are co-conspirators."

"Thank you very much."

"Your plan is well thought out. Even so...who can say whether she'll accept it."

"Sir?"

"No, it's nothing." I could only hope this fear of mine was ungrounded. "For the time being, we'll need to convince Claire to take you on as her maid."

"I'll leave that to you."

"Why *does* she reject you so thoroughly, though?"

"Ah... I suppose I express my love for her a bit too excitedly."

"Is that so?" I didn't quite understand what she meant, but Claire rarely expressed her true self around others like she did with Rae. Claire could be willful, but she knew how to keep up the appearance of a proper noble. "Can I ask you for one more thing, Rae Taylor?"

"If it is within my means to grant it."

"Be a good friend to Claire. She takes after me in that she is poorly equipped to articulate her feelings. As far as I know, she only opens up to Lene." There was another with whom Claire could be herself, but I had never quite liked that girl's inscrutability. Neither could I recall the last time I'd seen her. But that wasn't important right now.

"Her friend...huh?"

"I'm aware you see her romantically, and that poses its own challenges, no? It'd be good to see you at least stay with her as her friend."

"Indeed..."

I would later come to regret my words for the way they hurt and bound Rae. But I knew nothing of the depths of her own troubles at that time.

Claire's POV

"**H**EY, CATHERINE? I was thinking it's about time I introduce you to Pepi and Loretta."

"Hm...?" a sleepy voice hummed in response.

It was early morning in my room at the academy dorm. Lene and that insufferable commoner would be coming soon, but for now it was just me and my roommate, Catherine.

Catherine had hair that was blonde, soft, and curly, as well as teal-colored eyes—both traits similar to my own. We'd known each other since we were young and were often mistaken for sisters due to our similar appearance.

"I said I was thinking it's about time I introduce you to Pepi and Loretta," I repeated.

"Why?" she replied with a sleepy drawl.

"What do you mean, 'why'? They're my friends. Why wouldn't I want to introduce you to them?"

"Mmm…" Catherine flopped over on my bed without giving me a clear yes or no. Her face would have had most people thinking she was simply too sleepy to respond, but having known her for quite a while now, I knew she was just too lazy to think. "Zzz…"

"I know you're not actually sleeping. It's obvious, really."

"There's no tricking you, huh? All right, I'll get up…" Catherine slowly straightened her body. "Morning, Claire."

"Good morning, Catherine."

"So, where's my reward for getting up?"

"Why would I give you a reward for doing that?"

"'Cause it was hard."

"What in the world… Fine, but just one."

"Yaaay. Aaah." Catherine opened her mouth wide. With a sigh, I took a single candy from the pot on her desk and tossed it into her mouth. "Mmm, nothing beats licorice."

"I can't stand the flavor myself."

"You're so childish, Claire."

"If you're so mature, then why don't you feed yourself instead of making me do it for you?"

"Mmm, naaah. You bought them for me, so it's only right that you feed them to me too."

Those candies were her favorite, so I'd bought some the other day when I went out to shop.

"Could you stop trying to change the topic?" I asked.

"Oops, was I too obvious?"

"Just how long do you think I've known you?" I'd met Catherine at around the point at which I was old enough to understand my surroundings, which had also been around the time my mother passed away—more than ten years now. "So? Can I introduce you?"

"Jeez, you're so hasty."

"No, you're just too leisurely!" Catherine had been the idle sort since forever. She was my polar opposite, as someone who preferred to get things done as soon as possible.

"Mmm...nah. I think I'll pass on meeting them."

"Why?"

"It'd only cause problems for you if people knew we knew each other," she said flatly. It was a self-deprecating thing to say, but she said it so plainly, as though it were simple truth. I didn't approve.

"And just what's wrong with our being friends?!"

"Well, our families get along super badly, for one."

"Certainly House Achard and House François may at times be at odds, but that has nothing to do with us."

Catherine's family, House Achard, was one of the four great powers of Bauer, as I touched on earlier. They had a storied history but were now the leaders of a faction of nobles whose power was waning. King l'Ausseil and Rod, first in line to the throne, had the backing of the nobility at present, but only because the strongest faction favored them. Simultaneously, the factions led by House François and House Achard were vying for control within noble circles, hence the friction between our families that Catherine alluded to. But even given all that, I still considered her a friend. I treasured her as one of my few confidants in the small world of noble society.

"Isn't Loretta your future sister-in-law anyway?" I asked.

"Mmm, I guess...?" Catherine's brother (of sorts) Kristoff was Loretta's fiancé. Marriages between nobles were heavily defined by power disputes, but that's a topic for another time. Just understand that it was strange that Catherine hadn't at least met her future sister-in-law. She continued, "I mean, I was born from a mistress, so it's kinda iffy if we'd count as in-laws."

"I didn't think you worried about that kind of thing."

"Oh, I don't. But my parents do."

"I see..."

There were some unseemly rumors about Catherine's father, Clément. It wasn't unusual for nobles to prize status and lineage, but I'd heard he went so far as to mistreat nobles of lower rank, to say nothing of commoners who lacked either prestige. My father was a stickler for status in his own right, but even he didn't condescend to lord over the weak. People like Clément simply didn't understand what it truly meant to be a noble. As proof of that...

I looked at Catherine's left leg, which ended at the knee. She had lost her leg in the same accident in which I'd lost my mother. She had been riding in the carriage with which my parents' vehicle had collided.

Her leg hadn't been beyond healing, however. Although House Achard had lost influence, it still held the rank of marquess. If they paid for it, Catherine could have received top-notch magical treatment. But her father, Clément, had chosen not to. According to rumor, he was opposed to the idea of spending money on the child of a mistress. So instead, Catherine's left leg had been amputated at the knee, and now she needed a cane to walk.

"Anyway, let's leave my introduction for another day," she said. "Jeez..."

Well, that was that. No matter how much I might have wanted to, I couldn't forcibly introduce her to Pepi and Loretta as—

"Good morning, Miss Claire."

"Your beloved has arrived!"

"Good morning, Lene. You can go home already, commoner."

"Oh, I just love how bashful you can be, Miss Claire!"

"I'm not bashful, just fed up with you!"

Lene and the rambunctious commoner arrived. The commoner was up to her usual nonsense; just trying to respond to her was a waste of breath.

"I don't see Catherine around. It'd be nice to at least get to see her one of these days."

"Oh yeah, she's never here, is she?"

Lene and the commoner looked at the now empty bed. The Catherine I had been talking to up until now was gone without a trace.

"No, she's here, just...hiding," I said.

"Ah, I see," Lene replied.

"Ohh, I heard about that from Lene, but I'm surprised I really can't see her."

Catherine specialized in invisibility magic, a power that erased one's presence. She always used it to hide whenever someone entered the room, and it was because of this magic that I couldn't force an introduction with Pepi and Loretta.

"Are we perhaps disliked? It's been a long time since I last laid eyes on Catherine," Lene said.

"Of course not," I said. "She's just a little...fickle."

"Or perhaps shy," the commoner suggested.

"You be quiet."

Truth be told, I didn't quite know why Catherine wanted to hide herself. She rarely attended classes because of her leg, but she had still managed to maintain decent grades and graduate junior high school. The unseen efforts she made were laudable. She might've been a little quirky, but she was a gifted girl.

I still haven't given up on introducing you to everyone. It was too cruel to live forever unperceived. I prayed in my heart that a day would come when Catherine could smile alongside many friends.

"Hm? What's that sound I hear?" I asked.

"I hear it too," Lene said.

I was walking along, having been invited to a tea party by a young lady affiliated with House François's faction, when I heard a beautiful melody. It was a bit too distant to make out clearly, but I thought it sounded like a harp.

"Ah..." The commoner seemed to realize something and grabbed my hand before I could question her. "This way, Miss Claire."

"Wh-what are you doing, commoner?!"

"Rae, the tea party's going to start soon!"

The commoner didn't stop at our protests, however, continuing to drag me along. She was always a bit assertive, but she rarely physically forced me in any way. What could have overcome her? "Just where are you taking me, commoner?"

"Shhh! Look over there."

We were somewhere in the academy's central courtyard, near an arbor by a small pond—a different arbor than the one Pepi, Loretta, and I preferred for our tea. There sat a silent, silver-haired boy.

"Master Thane..."

"My...what a lovely sound."

Lene and I were overcome with admiration. It was a well-known fact that Thane was musically gifted, but this was the first I'd directly heard him play. The song he played was neither energetic nor bombastic but a sorrowful tune that resonated deeply with me.

As a noble, I too was educated in music, at least somewhat. I could manage to play most melodies on the piano as long as I had the score before me—but that was all. Thane's skill went far beyond that. The music I heard in that moment contained the self-expression of a bona fide artist.

"How marvelous, Master Thane!" Unable to wait any longer, I ran over to him. I thought I caught the commoner saying something behind me, but I didn't hear nor care what she said—praising Thane's wonderful performance took precedence, after all.

Thane's fingers stopped as he gave me a cold look. "...You're that François girl."

I was a bit hurt that he didn't recall my name. Nevertheless, I wasn't the type to falter because of that. "It's Claire. I'd be honored if you'd remember."

"Ah. Right, Claire," Thane said with disinterest and began to put his harp away.

"Are you finished already? I'd love to hear more."

"No... This is just a meaningless pastime of mine. My music isn't something worth sharing with others."

"I disagree. You were wonderful just now," Lene said, backing me up. She wasn't as learned in music as I, but even an amateur could tell Thane was wonderfully gifted.

"Even if that were true, music's only good for listening to. It has nothing to do with the qualities of a king," Thane spat bitterly as he finished putting away his harp. He held himself to a high standard. He was only second in line for the throne, but he constantly honed himself in case he needed to step up one day. He aspired to be like King l'Ausseil, frequently praised for his wisdom—although rumor had it that the two didn't quite get along.

I truly enjoyed hearing Thane play. Hearing him say it was just a meaningless pastime didn't sit right with me, not when he was so talented.

"Well then, how about we play a game that tests whether one has the qualities of a king?" the commoner said.

Thane raised an eyebrow. "You're Rae Taylor. I heard you became Claire's maid."

So he remembered her *name but not mine...* I was struck with a deep sense of humiliation. *First Master Rod and Master Yu, now Master Thane? Just what do they all see in this commoner?*

"You heard right. Being her maid brings me great happiness every single day."

"Enough of that," said Thane. "What's this game you speak of? The one that tests one's kingly qualities? Is it chess? I've heard you're quite skilled." Thane was doubtless referring to that time the commoner had played chess against Rod. News of how she'd gone toe-to-toe with him had spread throughout the academy for a time, but I was surprised to hear word had reached even Thane's ears.

"Not chess. It's a game called the King's Game," the commoner said. I personally hadn't heard of it before.

"Hmm... Sounds interesting. How do you play?" It seemed Thane, despite his extensive knowledge, hadn't heard of it either.

The commoner explained the rules. First, we drew lots. Then the one who drew the winning lot gave an order for the other players to follow.

"And this really measures the qualities of a king?" Thane asked.

"It does."

"Very well... I'll play."

The commoner rolled up strips of paper and wrote numbers on the ends, creating lots for us to draw. She then held the strips so we couldn't see the numbers. "Please draw, everyone."

We each drew, starting with Thane, then me, and lastly Lene. The fourth lot remained in the commoner's hand.

"All right, who's the king?" the commoner called.

"What are you on about?" Thane asked, slightly bewildered.

"This is how the game is played. We all say, 'Who's the king,' and check the numbers we drew at the same time."

What a strange game, I thought.

"I see," Thane mused.

"All right. Ready, everyone?"

All together, we said: "Who's the king?"

Our first king was—

"Me, it seems." Thane.

"What's your order then, Master Thane?"

"Hmm... Yes, well..." Thane hemmed and hawed. As kind as he was, he was likely thinking carefully to pick an order that wasn't too extreme. "How about number two and number three hold hands?"

"Number two, that's me!" the commoner declared.

"Guh... I'm number three." Just why did bad things have to happen to good people?

"Hold out your hand, please, Miss Claire."

"I suppose I have no choice."

The commoner grabbed my outreached hand. Her palm was surprisingly smooth for a commoner. Perhaps she had a skin-care routine. How cheeky.

"Eek!" I shrieked. "Wh-wh-what are you doing?!"

The commoner was rubbing the back of my palm with her thumb.

"Just admiring the smoothness of your skin."

"Just hold my hand like normal! This is sufficient, yes? Let's move on!" I hurried things along, letting go of her hand.

"All right, round two—"

"Who's the king?" we all said again.

The second king was—

"M-me?" Lene. As a commoner, she seemed a bit hesitant at the thought of potentially ordering royalty around. After pondering for an even longer time than Thane, she said, "Number four, please stroke the head of number two."

Thane paused. "I'm number four."

"A-and I'm number two." My heart began to race. Thane, my dear Thane, was going to stroke my head? *Oh goodness.*

"I don't believe a woman's hair should be stroked so frivolously..." said Thane.

"But, Master Thane, we must follow the rules," the commoner said.

"But..."

"I'm fine with it, Master Thane," I said, perhaps a bit strongly. I couldn't let this opportunity slip by, after all.

"Well then...I apologize for this."

I closed my eyes as Thane's fingers, the very ones that had produced such beautiful music earlier, reached toward me. With some hesitation, he touched my hair and stroked.

"Aah..." According to some, touching the hair of someone of the opposite gender is a more intimate act than whispering confessions of love in one's own bedchambers. In other words, we were practically—

No, calm yourself, Claire François! You're in front of Master Thane. This is no time to get lost in your fantasies.

"That should be enough. Let's begin the next round." The moment didn't last more than ten seconds, but Thane's face was red as his hand retreated. How cute.

"Right. Okay, round three—"

"Who's the king?" we said again.

The third king was—

"Oh, it's me." The commoner, the one most unfit to be king. I felt a shiver run down my spine. Just what unreasonable demand would she give? "Number two and number four, please kiss."

"What...?" asked Thane.

"Wh-what did you just say, commoner?!" I was number four, and from his reaction, I could presume that number two was Thane. *Huh? Huh?! Is this happening?!*

"This is going too far," Thane said.

"Th-that's right," I politely agreed, though I had been slightly—*very slightly*—hoping something might happen. There was a proper order to these things, you see...

"What? But the king's commands are absolute. Chop chop, now, thank you."

"I see..."

"Master Thane?!" I exclaimed, having completely lost all semblance of calm. *He's going to kiss me? In front of everybody?!*

"Now kiss!" said the commoner.

"No."

"Master Thane...?" I asked.

Thane's voice was stern, his expression angry. "Just what about this game tests the qualities of a king?" he demanded of the commoner, glaring at her. "Are you mocking me?" His eyes warned her to choose her next words carefully.

The commoner seemed calm now, but she had clearly been rude to him—and as my maid, her actions were my responsibility. I hated to leave such a bad impression on him, but as a noble, I had my obligations. "Master Thane," I said, "please allow me to apologize for this affront—"

"I just knew you would figure it out, Master Thane!" the commoner said, cutting me off.

"What...?" Thane stared at her in disbelief.

"The real purpose of this game was to see whether or not you would ascertain the truth," she said nonchalantly. "If you, Master Thane, had accepted that order without question, it would have proven you lacked the qualities of a worthy monarch."

"You were testing...*me*?"

"Do forgive me. But I thought you deserved proof that you truly do have the qualities of a king, Master Thane."

Thane fell silent, his expression conflicted. The commoner claimed he embodied these qualities, but what value did such praise have when it came from the likes of her?

"I'm leaving," he said after a pause.

"Master Thane!" I called, worried.

Expressionless, Thane stood and left the arbor without punishing the commoner. He was as moody as ever, but that was part of what made him so lovable.

"Rae..."

"Yes, Lene?"

"Is what you just said true?"

"Oh no, I just wanted to tease Miss Claire."

Wh-what?! "C-commoner, you...!" She had gone too far this time!

"Miss Claire?"

"What?" I said, cross.

"How did it feel to have your hair stroked by Thane?"

I let out a meaningless sound out of sheer embarrassment. *Ah, jeez! Obviously it felt amazing!*

"...And that's what happened."

"Aw, how nice! I wish I could've heard Thane play the harp too!"

"Me three!"

I was joined at the arbor after school by Lene, Pepi, Loretta, and the commoner. We had gone there for tea quite often as of late, with we three nobles served by my maids. On the table was fragrant tea and a variety of sweets, all of which I had procured from the top-of-the-line restaurant Broumet, much to Pepi and Loretta's delight.

We had chatted about a variety of things thus far and had moved on to discussing my recent encounter with Thane.

I asked, "Do you two also find Thane's playing exquisite?"

"Absolutely!"

"Of course."

Pepi and Loretta were far more versed in music than I. Pepi was gifted with the violin, and Loretta with the piano. They'd even won awards for their performances in Bauer.

"Come to think of it, we first met thanks to music, didn't we?" I said.

Loretta blushed. "Just remembering that day makes me want to curl up into a ball of shame..."

"It's nothing to be embarrassed about. You're a brilliant performer now, aren't you?" Pepi said encouragingly. Their relationship hadn't changed since I first met them.

My mind drifted back to the memory.

Words of praise came from all directions the second after I played the final note.

"Well done, Miss Claire. That was wonderful."

"I'm honored, Miss Carol."

After being praised by the performance instructor, Carol Achard, I left the piano. The other students and I were in the Royal Academy's junior high music room taking our first piano lessons as junior high students. Music was an essential part of a noble's education, and the piano was the basics of basics. I'd been given strict piano lessons since my girlhood, so playing an étude of that level of complexity was child's play to me.

"That was amazing, Miss Claire!"

"You sounded so good!"

"Not at all. I'm sure everyone can manage such a thing." I wasn't being modest; I genuinely believed that what I'd done wasn't praiseworthy. Most of the students had been trained by home tutors like I had. To stumble on a simple étude would have brought shame to any noble. Of course, I doubted any of the increasingly common lowborn students would be able to do the same, but that was just their way.

"Loretta, you're up next. Please come to the front," Carol said with a kind smile.

A girl with short black hair and brown eyes stood up. She walked forward with grace, likely from having dabbled in some form of martial art. A wide smile was on her freckled face, wide enough to make me wonder just what she could be so happy about.

"There's no need to be nervous. Now go ahead and play."

"Okay!"

The girl—Loretta, her name was—took a deep breath, put her hands on the keys, and began. Her performance was...lacking. She played the wrong notes a number of times, was off tempo, and clearly lacked proper technique.

"How awful. And she's supposed to be a noble?"

"She must not have received a proper education, the poor thing."

I heard some snickers from the students around me. Certainly Loretta's performance was far from *good*, but it was improper to speak ill behind someone's back. Disgruntled, I could only hope she didn't hear any of their words.

And it seemed she didn't, for she was completely engrossed in playing. While Loretta's skill might have been lacking, her enjoyment of the act was clearly anything but. After finishing, she took her fingers off the keys with obvious reluctance.

"Very good. You still have a ways to go, but it's clear you enjoy the piano," Carol Achard said.

"Yes, I love it!"

"Wonderful. There's nothing more important than enjoying something. But this étude is still a bit difficult for you. Let's practice with something easier for now."

"Yes, ma'am!" Loretta bowed deeply before returning to her seat.

"Pepi, you're up next. Please come to the front."

"Right away."

I watched Loretta as the next student was called, wondering to myself whether I had ever found piano as pleasurable as she did.

"Aren't you at all ashamed of how bad you are?"

"You were terrible. The difference between you and Miss Claire is the difference between heaven and earth."

Having forgotten something in the classroom, I returned after classes and found a number of students surrounding two girls. One of the girls, Loretta, was cowering on the ground while the other girl—Pepi, if I recalled her name correctly—stood before her.

"Who do you think you are, ganging up on someone?!" Pepi was about as intimidating as an angry kitten, but her anger was certainly real. "Just watch, one day Loretta will be the kingdom's greatest pianist!"

"Aha ha ha! You hear that? This girl seriously thinks she can become a master pianist one day!"

"When she can't even play a mid-level étude?"

"Talentless trash like her? No way!"

"Shut up, shut up, shut up!"

The surrounding students continued to tease Loretta. Pepi defended her as hard as she could, but Loretta was beginning to cry.

It appeared I had walked in on some bullying. This activity was by no means a rare occurrence in the small world that was noble society, but I wasn't particularly fond of it.

"Oh my," I said. "Is pure talent the only thing you lot know how to judge? Do the words 'growth' and 'effort' simply not exist in your dictionaries?"

"M-Miss Claire..." The bullies flinched upon seeing me arrive.

I continued, "House Kugret is a military house. Would Loretta not make quick work of you in a battle of magic or martial arts?"

"Ah..." The bullies seemed to consider this for a moment. Our school, of course, incorporated mock combat into its curriculum.

"Moreover, it's utter nonsense to claim Loretta has no talent. She's hugely talented in the most important regard." Loretta frowned at me, even more confused than the bullies. I turned to her. "Lady Carol said it herself: You *like* piano, perhaps more than any of us, and that is what truly matters here."

"Oh..."

"Or were those empty words you said?"

"Absolutely not! I...I truly do love piano!" Loretta nodded so vigorously that I thought her neck might snap.

One of the bullies said, "B-but just liking something doesn't mean—"

"Have you heard of the phrase 'passion over effort'?"

"Huh?"

"U-um, I can't say I have..."

Of course not, I thought. *Or you wouldn't be doing something so foolish.*

"Anyone can put in effort if they put their mind to enduring unpleasantness. But forced effort pales in comparison to those who endeavor out of pure enjoyment."

"And you believe she has passion?"

"That's up to Loretta to decide. But wouldn't it be all the more thrilling that way?"

The bullies shared an awkward glance.

"Let's go."

"R-right."

"Yeah..."

One by one, they made themselves scarce.

"Thank you, Miss Claire," Pepi said.

"I only stated the truth, no more. Rather, I'm impressed you were so brave as to stand against so many."

"Loretta's my friend. It's my dream to play violin at a concert with her piano accompanying me."

So these girls were childhood friends. That made them like Catherine and me. "You'd do well to treasure that bond," I said. "Nothing's more important to us aristocrats."

"Right!"

"Loretta," I said.

"Y-yes!" she answered.

"I, Claire François, have gone out on a limb to support you. Take care that you do not make me a liar."

"Yes, ma'am!"

"Good." I pulled her to her feet. "You two are promising. Consider yourselves mine from this day forward."

"Who would have thought that bullied girl would go on to become one of our generation's most celebrated pianists? Even those bullies are your fans now."

"You're doing quite well yourself, Pepi. Don't you have a solo concert coming up? That's incredible!"

My friends praised each other proudly.

"I'm surprised those bullies have the nerve to be your fans after all they did to you," I said.

"Ah ha ha, well, it's all in the past. It doesn't bother me anymore," said Loretta.

"That's a little too forgiving, don't you think?" Pepi said.

Nevertheless, if Loretta felt it was water under the bridge, then that was that.

"In the end, it seems I was right to see the promise in you two," I said, satisfied.

"You see promise in me too, right?" said the commoner. "Does that mean great things await in my future?"

"Since when have I ever said I see promise in you?!" I scolded her.

"I really am grateful to you, though, Miss Claire," said Pepi. "We might have given up if not for your help then."

"Yeah. Thank you, Miss Claire," said Loretta.

There was no need for them to thank me, of course. I had merely expressed displeasure at unsightly behavior and moved to claim what caught my eye as my own, nothing more.

"Oh, don't be so formal," I said. "You two are my dear frien—*ahem*, belong to me, don't you?"

"Yeah, guys. No need to be so distant when we're all friends!"

"Why are *you* acting like you're friends with us?!" we all exclaimed at the commoner.

I had almost said something deeply embarrassing, but I was fortunately able to conceal it by lashing out at the commoner.

"Hey, Rae? Are you what they call homosexual?" Misha asked while we were eating lunch in the cafeteria. Her question was so sudden and direct that I choked for a moment.

"Misha?" I said around a cough. "Just what good could come of asking such a question?"

"Miss Misha, I don't think that's something one ought to ask in public," said Lene.

We both agreed the subject was best avoided.

"I don't mind," the commoner said. "Do you really want to know?"

"As your best friend, yes," said Misha.

They continued indifferently, paying no mind to Lene or to me. I didn't particularly care to find out the commoner's sexual preferences, but, well, I supposed I was a little curious.

"Hmm... Well, I can't be totally sure, but I'm probably gay. I've never had that special kind of feeling for a guy," she said rather idly.

I knew it. My suspicions had been justified all along.

I inched away from the commoner. She noticed and inched the same distance closer, so I inched farther.

"Why are you moving away from me?" she asked.

"I fear for my virtue."

"Oh, c'mon. I'm not going to do anything."

"So you say..."

It was unnatural to lust after someone of the same gender. Was it truly safe to keep her by my side as a maid? Was my purity not in danger?

To my surprise, Misha asked, "Is the way you're acting not unjustly prejudiced, Miss Claire?"

"How so?"

"Think about it. You're heterosexual, are you not?"

"Well, of course," I said. *How absurd. I could never fall in love with a wom... Oh. W-wait, no, that was a misunderstanding! I thought she was a boy at the time, so it doesn't count! Though if she were willing, then maybe... N-no, what are you thinking, Claire François?!*

"You like Master Thane, right?" the commoner teased.

I felt like she'd known of my love for him from the very start. Just how could she have come by such information, though?

"Rae, be quiet for a minute," Misha chided. "Miss Claire, how would you feel if a boy told you not to make sexual advances toward him?"

"How dare he think me so depraved!"

"Exactly. But you're saying similar things to Rae."

"Oh..." I'd had no idea I harbored such biases. Being homosexual simply meant that one felt affection for those of the same gender; nothing else really distinguished such people from anyone else. Homosexuals weren't necessarily more lustful or predatory than other people... That didn't mean the commoner's daily behavior toward me was *entirely* appropriate, but still.

"W-well...gender's not all that important when it comes to love, right? It just so happens that the person Rae loves is a girl," Lene said, trying to lighten the awkward mood.

"Nope!" the commoner said.

"Huh?"

"Gender *is* important!"

"O-oh, really?"

The commoner then explained that Lene's supposition was yet another common misconception about homosexuals. It was so obvious when I thought about it—being *homo*sexual inherently meant that one wasn't interested in the other gender. The "love is blind" narrative, in which people fell in love regardless of gender, made for a good story, but it didn't reflect real homosexuals that well. In fact, it was perhaps even a tad offensive.

"I see. I didn't know that either," Misha said.

"Well, I can't blame any of you for that. There really isn't much opportunity to learn," the commoner replied.

Unlike the Nur Empire, where same-sex marriage was recognized, public homosexuality was relatively uncommon in Bauer. The biases I held were fairly widespread, and not many people even tried to understand homosexuals. Novels and plays often depicted them as lecherous, just as I'd assumed, or as idealized romantics, as Lene had—but those beliefs were swiftly overturned the moment one actually spoke with a person who truly lived those experiences.

"Is there any objectionable behavior we ought to change?" Misha softly asked. It was plain to see that she cared for her friend and was trying to better understand her.

"No, not really. I'm happy enough just being able to dote on Miss Claire every day."

"It's because you're always saying those sorts of things that I worry for my chastity!" I was newly aware of my prejudices, but the commoner didn't help her case when she was always so brazenly forward with her affections. She practically invited misunderstanding.

"Yeaaah, but I just can't go on without making a joke of it all," the commoner said with a weak grin.

No... Perhaps the frailty I saw in that moment was only my imagination, but her smile certainly did seem more fleeting than usual.

"Rae...you..." Misha gave the commoner a worried look.

"Relax, relax, I'm fine. I'm used to my love going unrequited."

The commoner claimed to love me, and as far as I could tell, she was genuine in her affection. But I could not reciprocate. There was nothing to be done about that sorry truth, yet my heart ached the slightest bit at the thought. I had grown used to dealing with her antics, had I not? So why did it pain me to think that I was unable to reciprocate her feelings?

"So you've given up on Miss Claire, Rae?" asked Misha.

"Trying to cover everything today, huh, Misha?" the commoner joked.

"I'm sorry if I'm making you uncomfortable."

"Not at all. To answer your question, hmm... Well, I guess I have given up in a way, but in another way, I haven't," she said ambiguously.

"What does that mean?" Lene asked.

"I don't expect Miss Claire to return my feelings. Miss Claire is interested in someone else, and I want to support her in that. I'm happy just being near her. That being said..."

"Yes?" I pressed.

"I haven't completely given up on you, Miss Claire. That would be impossible, ah ha ha." The commoner laughed, but no one joined in.

For a brief—ever so brief—moment, I had the urge to hug her.

"At any rate, Miss Claire, please continue to act the way you always have. I'm actually quite happy with our current arrangement."

"I see..."

"Of course, you're welcome to fall in love with me at any time."

"I will not." I steeled my heart as best I could as I shot her down.

"Aw, figures... All right, let's leave the heavy stuff at that," she said. "Shall we go have our usual flirting session now, Miss Claire?"

"Absolutely not, and don't make it sound like that's something we do!"

"Oh, c'mon. You know you want to."

"Save the sleep talk for when you're in bed!" I retorted.

"Ah ha ha ha."

From then on, the two of us continued as we always did. The commoner teased me, Lene soothed me, and Misha watched on. Just like always. But something about my perspective on the commoner changed, just a bit. I wondered to myself just how many times this girl, who always acted like a buffoon, had been hurt.

"Miss Claire?"

"What?"

"You hate me, right?"

The commoner knew my answer, yet she asked anyway. So I gave her what she wanted to hear: "Of course I do."

"Aw, figures." She smiled, satisfied with my response. "But even so, I still love you."

Even if you know that your love won't be returned...?

"Shucks. If only I could fall in love with another lesbian," she muttered, sounding as carefree as always.

Yet once again, her words made my heart hurt.

2

The Cheeky Maid and Me

"**A**ND SO, the Academy Knights selection test will be held again this year for those who are interested."

One Saturday morning, we sat in a lecture room listening to the current commander of the Academy Knights, Lorek Kugret. As you might have guessed from his surname, he was Loretta's brother. The Kugrets were a military family with the noble rank of earl, and they were one of many families who held important posts in the army. As one of the first families to realize the importance of magic, they had sought instruction from Torrid Magic—a man who had greatly advanced the kingdom's study of the arcane—and thereby maintained their influence through the changing times.

Lorek himself was a frank but kind person, set to be the next head of his family. Loretta was similar in personality, I supposed, although I'd say she was somewhat more laid-back.

The Academy Knights to which Lorek referred was a self-governed organization within the Royal Academy. It comprised select students from the academy, traditionally from royal and high-standing noble families, and the highest-ranked among them were given authority equal to a teacher's. The Academy Knights acted as both student council and disciplinary committee, and they were expected to protect the school in emergencies—as the "knight" part of their name implied.

"You already know I'll be taking that test." Rod was the first to volunteer. Understandable, given his personality.

"I'll take it too," Yu said, raising his hand. Despite his elegant, nigh feminine looks, he was one of the academy's strongest fighters, and for that he was even called the "Prince of Ice." His aptitude in magic wasn't particularly striking, but he had been trained in close quarters combat since his youth.

"C'mon, you're taking it too, Thane."

"Fine... Such a pain..." With Rod's urging, Thane reluctantly raised his hand. Given his personality, Thane probably didn't care much for these group activities, but as a prince he had a responsibility to join.

"I appreciate the participation of the princes. Anyone else?" Lorek said.

"I'll be taking it as well." I raised my hand and volunteered myself, as was only to be expected.

"Miss Claire, huh? Are you sure? This test might be a bit much for a woman."

"Nonsense. Certainly I may not be as strong as a man, but I am more than qualified when it comes to magic as well as the administration of clerical tasks." Everyone in House Francois had joined the ranks of the Academy Knights as a student, including my father *and* my mother. I was naturally expected to live up to their legacy.

Lorek hesitated for a moment, but being the capable leader he was, he soon gave his assent.

"In that case, I'd like to take the test as well." From my side, the commoner volunteered too. I made no effort to conceal my distaste.

"You're only wasting your time," I said.

"Oh really? Remind me, who was it who lost to me in every subject except etiquette on our last round of tests?"

"Why, you...! I won't lose this time, just you watch!" How could she be so haughty after only winning once?! "Misha, you take the test too. If by some odd chance the commoner passes, she'll need someone to rein her in."

"I'm not Rae's keeper..." Misha said unenthusiastically. Nevertheless, she raised her hand and reluctantly volunteered.

A number of other students raised their hands as well. Lorek wrote down their names and distributed an outline for the assessment. "The test will begin tomorrow morning. There will be two subjects: clerical work and magic. Details are listed on the outlines I just handed out; please check them yourselves. Now, please excuse me."

With that, he left the room.

"Hmph. Someone as lowly as you could never become an Academy Knight." I scoffed at the commoner beside me, though I had to wonder why she looked so happy to be insulted.

"All right! You three are taking the test too? This is gonna be a good time," Rod said.

"Let's do our best, Thane," Yu said.

"Hmph. I couldn't care less how I do," Thane said.

The three princes came over. Rod looked full of confidence, Yu looked just confident enough, and Thane looked entirely apathetic.

"You're surprisingly dedicated, Rae," Misha said. "Although I get the feeling the Academy Knights aren't the object of your dedication."

"Yep. I just want to be with Miss Claire."

"I knew it." Misha sighed, defeated. She seemed pretty on edge about taking the Academy Knights test, but knowing her personality, she would doubtless hold nothing back and give it her all.

"Master Rod, do you know how the tests will proceed? All Lorek said was that there were clerical and magical components," I said. As I mentioned earlier, it was common knowledge that all generations of the royal family had joined the Academy Knights. There was a chance Rod had an idea of what we could expect to face.

"You know I can't tell you that, it'd be unfair. You'll find out tomorrow anyway, and it's not like one day is really enough time to prepare anything."

"I suppose that's true." That being said, this was a test, which meant this was a perfect opportunity... I glared sharply at the commoner. "Commoner, let's have ourselves another competition!"

On top of the commoner's head, Ralaire bounced in surprise. Ralaire was a baby water slime the commoner had tamed. It was a monster, but it was also...so, so terribly cute. Just wonderfully, *incredibly* cute. Every single move it made was utterly *overflowing* with cuteness.

But I digress.

"If you don't make it into the Academy Knights, then you will leave the academy," I said.

"What? No way, I don't want to."

"Again, at least consider it!" I could have sworn this commoner was only good for wearing away my patience...

"Fine," she said. "Then let's use the same conditions as the last test."

I was about to agree, then stopped. "Wait a minute. Are you trying to deceive me again?" Last time, I had fallen for the commoner's cheap tricks. I wasn't about to fall for them again.

"Oh please, I wouldn't be that mean. How about this? If I fail, you lose. If I pass, I win."

"I suppose that'd be fine... Wait, no! I'd lose either way!" I just couldn't let my guard down with her.

"Fine. If I fail, you win. If I pass, I win."

"Can't it be that I win if I pass?"

"But you'll definitely pass, Miss Claire. That would make it too easy for you to win."

My mood lifted a bit with her words. Perhaps she was starting to learn her place? "Fine. So, what do you want if you win?"

"The same as before. You will grant me a single favor."

"Very well."

"Then our little competition is on."

Just like last time, we swore to God before Misha.

"Oh ho ho! I'll have you out of this academy once and for all soon enough, commoner." I rolled out a laugh full of confidence and pointed a finger her way.

We were at one of the many training grounds at the academy. The commoner and I had breezed through the first part of the Academy Knights selection test and were now moving on to the second and final test: mock combat. Nine matches had already been held, leaving my match with her as the last one left.

"I doubt it, but let's try and have fun anyway." The commoner seemed perfectly composed, even though I stood directly before her.

Hmph, look at you getting all conceited just because you're a dual-caster, I thought. "Fun? Oh please. You won't even have the leeway to enjoy yourself, you lowly commoner."

"Heh heh, if you say so, Miss Claire. Good luck."

"Grrr...!" I fumed. The commoner simply wouldn't stop trying to make a fool out of me. But now I could put her in her place.

"Combatants, are you ready?"

"Ready."

"Yes."

"Then let the final match...begin!"

I cautiously readied my wand and waited for the commoner to make the first move. But she didn't, instead taking a slack stance with her wand and observing me.

"Are you not going to attack?" I asked.

"I was about to ask you the same."

"I'm allowing you the first move out of pity."

"Oh, is that so?"

Even after our short exchange, the commoner didn't make a move.

"Well, we can't very well have a battle if nobody makes a move," I said.

"That's fine by me; I'm happy enough just gazing at you."

"Don't you ever get tired of trying to play games with me?!"

Fine, then I'll make the first—

However, no sooner had I begun to think that than she said, "But we can't stand around forever, can we? I'll start, then." She raised her right arm. "Enclose."

My vision was immediately obstructed by something. Faster than I could process, I was encased in a cage, presumably summoned by her earth-attribute magic.

I was being *mocked*.

"Hmph. Is this all you've got?" I pierced the cage with flame spears, melting the walls, and hopped out. With a sigh, I brushed the dust off my shoulders.

Then the commoner made her next move. "How about just a little more teasing to start?" She created small arrows of stone and fired them at me.

"Useless." With a wide, horizontal swing of my arm, I summoned a wall of flame to melt away her arrows. "Not terrible, if I do say so myself."

"Far from it—that was wonderful, Miss Claire!"

"Hmph. I suppose I'll take the offensive now." I raised a hand and envisioned a large spear, the fire-attribute spell Flame Lance. The spell only required medium aptitude to cast, but it became far, far more powerful when used by someone with a higher aptitude, such as myself. From above my raised, spread palm, a spear about the size of a jousting lance appeared. "Ah, yes. As a noble, everything I do—even magic—must be art."

"You're amazing, Miss Claire! The aesthetics are a little enh, but what a wonderful display of control!"

"Oh, will you be quiet!" I snapped. *H-hmph! What does a commoner know of art, anyway? It doesn't look* that *bad, does it...?* "Disappear!"

I swung my arm down, sending my Flame Lance speeding toward the commoner. She tried to raise a wall of earth to defend herself.

"Fool! Did you forget how I melted your magic earlier?!" My Flame Lance was in a league of its own, far stronger than the versions other casters could produce. On top of that, the earth attribute was weak to fire. My attack was sure to pierce her defenses.

Or so I thought...

"It's not melting?! Why?!" The strange metallic wall of earth the commoner created withstood my attack. "I suppose superaptitude magic is nothing to laugh at, even in the hands of a fool..."

"I'm honored."

"But how much longer can you keep that up?" I created another spear of flame and purposely fired it to miss. "Turn!"

I manipulated the lance so it would trace back to the commoner's blind spot, but she was no pushover. She created another wall behind her and blocked my attack. Even so, I was ready.

"Burst!" Just before the spear contacted the wall, I snapped my fingers, causing the spear to scatter into a shower of tiny bullets that circled above and rained down on the commoner. Confident, I declared my victory. "I've got you now!"

"Aw, so close." But the commoner somehow dispersed my magic with strange bullets of her own.

"You've gotta be kidding me. That fast?" Rod said, equally stunned in his admiration.

"Argh... How can a commoner be this strong?"

"What's wrong, Miss Claire? Giving up already?"

"No way." I prepared my next attack. "Allow me to apologize beforehand, Master Rod."

"Hm?"

I abandoned the thought of using fire spears and instead pelted the commoner with a large number of fire bullets, a weaker form of magic. The commoner protected herself with her strange metal wall, but that was part of my plan.

"I'm not done yet!" I continued to rain down fire bullets without pause.

"I see," Yu said in understanding. Indeed, I was trying to deprive the commoner of oxygen like Rod had with Misha in their mock battle. No matter how strong the commoner's defenses were, she wouldn't be able to resist if I continually burned away all her breathable air.

I'M IN LOVE WITH THE VILLAINESS

Or so I had thought.

"Okay then, how about this?" The commoner moved her tight barrier outward to push back my fire bullets and secure fresh air. She then moved her barriers out even farther, this time maneuvering them to enclose me.

"Oh no you don't!" I cried.

She was trying to repeat her first attack, but I wasn't about to let her. I outran the barrier and avoided its enclosure, then distanced myself from her.

"It's not quite as flashy as our battle, but it's still quite impressive on a technical level," Rod said.

"Yes, you're absolutely right," Misha agreed.

I overheard the others commenting on our fight, and truth be told, I hadn't expected the commoner to last nearly this long. I supposed she wasn't a top student for nothing. "Cheeky little thing..." I muttered under my breath.

"What are you going to show me next, Miss Claire?" she called.

"What insolence." I raised both my arms. In the air appeared four crests—the crests of House François. "I can't believe I'm using this on a commoner... Light!"

A beam of light shot forth from each crest on my command, streaking past the commoner on either side and searing the ground. She was visibly tense after that—as was only proper.

"That was just a warning shot," I said. This magic was my trump card, the high-aptitude spell Magic Ray. Due to its lethality, I'd only ever brought it out a few times. "I may only be able to shoot it a limited number of times, but its power should be readily apparent. You may have your barrier, but if I by chance land a direct blow, you're not coming away unscathed. Surrender."

Confident in my victory, I demanded that she yield. She might have been an intolerable commoner, but I had no interest in hurting her, if it could be avoided.

"Hmm... That does look pretty dangerous, but..."

"But?"

"Why would I surrender when I could just win?"

I stared in utter disbelief—when suddenly I was staring upward.

"Eek?!" I realized I had been dropped down a hole that had formed in the ground. It had been about five meters deep at first, but it was getting deeper by the second. "Commoner! How dare you use such boorish magic against me!"

"But it's effective, right?"

While I hated to do so, I had to agree that it was. It would have been one thing if I could move through the air like Thane, but I was helpless against this pitfall attack. Fire-attribute magic had no way to create footholds, and trying to propel myself straight up was risky, with the hole being so narrow. If I had water-attribute magic, I'd have been able to fill the hole slowly and float my way up, but it would have been hard to outpace the speed with which the hole was deepening, not to mention that I would risk drowning.

Nevertheless, could I really allow myself to be done in by such...such *uncouth* magic?! "I refuse to accept this defeat!"

"Then try and escape."

"Oh, I will! Just you wait, I'll widen this hole with my magic, and—"

"Claire...give it up." That was when my ambitions were cut short by the refreshing voice of Thane, who had been silent up until now.

"What are you saying, Master Thane? I can still fight!"

"You haven't noticed...? Rae still hasn't used a single water spell, the attribute strongest against your fire."

I gasped in shock. The commoner had super-aptitude magic in both water and earth attributes, but not once during our fight had she used a single water spell. "You...were going easy on me?"

"Yep!"

"You...! You were toying with me the whole time!"

"Do you want to keep going?"

"Of course I do!" My blood was boiling, and I was about to melt away all the surrounding earth when—

"You got this, Miss Claire!" the commoner encouraged me.

"You're insufferable, you know that?!" I melted away some earth, but the stubborn commoner just replaced it with more. "Nnnnnnnnn*gaaahhhh*!" I was gradually losing my cool. I hadn't expected such a wide difference in skill between us. Even so, I had known about her aptitude beforehand, so it was on me for not coming up with appropriate countermeasures.

There has to be something *left for me to do...!* As shameless as it was to say, I considered myself the best of the best. I hadn't felt so weak in a long, long time. I couldn't even recall the last time I'd been rendered so powerless.

No... I remember... A dull recollection came to mind, faint but sure, of the time I'd lost my mother. I had been powerless then too, at the mercy of cruel reality.

I'd rather take the risk than have to feel so hopeless again! I knew it was dicey, but I decided to try to propel myself straight up out of the hole. It was better than doing nothing. I steeled myself, then concentrated my magic on my feet and—

"I'm sorry, Miss Claire, but I'm going to call this match. The winner is Rae," Lorek said.

"I can't accept this!"

"Misssss Claaaaaire!"

"I know, I know. What do you want this time?"

Passing the test wasn't a matter of winning our matches but whether we performed admirably, so in the end, both the commoner and I managed to join the Academy Knights. As soon as we received the crests that proved we had been inducted, the commoner came running to me with glee. Her methods might have been questionable, but a loss was a loss. I would do whatever favor she demanded of me, as per our agreement.

At least, I had prepared myself to.

"My request is the same as before," she said.

"Huh?"

"Whatever happens, please don't give up."

"Wait, why? I already promised that last time." This made no sense. As far as I understood this girl, she was the kind of person to use a chance to demand *anything* of me to satiate her lust.

"I know, but the same thing is fine with me. Please promise me again."

"I don't mind, but...you're sure?"

"Yes."

"Fine, then... I, Claire François, swear to God to never give up. I promise never to abandon hope and to keep going until the end."

"Thank you." The commoner smiled, seeming deeply satisfied for some reason. I just couldn't make sense of her. "Miss Claire, I'm hungry. Let's go to the cafeteria."

I sighed. "I'm surprised you can act so indifferent after beating me in such a shameless way."

"Thank you so much! I did my best!"

"I wasn't praising you!"

I swore to myself that I would win our next little competition when she said, "Please never change, Miss Claire."

"Huh? What prompted that?"

"Ah, don't worry, it's nothing. Let's go, Miss Claire."

"Wha—hey! Who do you think you're touching, commoner?!"

The commoner's expression seemed a bit clouded as she grabbed my hand and made for the cafeteria. Even after all this time, I still couldn't understand her.

"To the 143rd generation of recruits to the Academy Knights! Cheers!"

"Cheers!"

The sound of clinking glasses filled the room. We were in the Academy Knight's exclusive meeting room. Typically the room was awash with paperwork, but that had been cleared away for today's celebration. The desks were lined with various platters of food, all a step down from what I was used to, but no doubt pleasant for your average noble. The commoner had beelined for the food right after the opening toast and was busy filling her plate.

"Goodness... How can you be so gluttonous? You realize this is technically a ceremony, right? The food's only here as a formality."

"Oh, c'mon. It'd be a waste not to enjoy it all. Especially when it's so good."

I looked at the commoner's plate and saw she had deftly piled it with a variety of breads, roast beef, and some marinated vegetables. Ralaire was on her head, nibbling away at a biscuit.

"Hmph. You might be fine with this food, but for anyone with a more sophisticated palate, like me—"

"Is the food not to your liking, Claire?"

"O-oh, Master Yu..."

Yu appeared just as I was mocking the commoner. His plate was, like the commoner's, generously piled with food. "The food's pretty good, you know? I mean, it isn't on the level of Broumet, but it's up there."

"Hell yeah it is. Commander Lorek really pulled out all the stops." Rod came over as well, his plate stacked with meat.

"Are you not going to eat, Claire...?" Thane asked, having come over as well. His plate was mostly vegetables.

"O-oh, I, uh..."

"Sorry for the wait, Miss Claire. Here is your food." Lene saved me from my predicament then, giving me a wink as she handed me a plate mostly consisting of baked sweets that had been beautifully arranged.

"Oh, so Lene was bringing your food," Yu said.

"Yes...yes, that's right!" I said. "I knew I could trust her to bring me a well-balanced meal."

"Makes sense. Not like a lady of House François would ever be so rude as to not partake of such a thoughtfully laid-out spread," Rod said.

"Indeed..." Thane said.

The three princes sounded convinced. I could always count on Lene, my ever excellent maid, to be there for me. *Unlike a certain incompetent, that is...*

I let out a sigh of relief right as Lorek came over. "Congratulations on joining the Academy Knights, Your Royal Highnesses, Miss Claire," he said. "And you two as well, Rae and Misha. I speak for all the knights when I say we're pretty thrilled to have such gifted members join our ranks." He let out a hearty laugh, coming off as rather unfamiliar with proper decorum. Surprisingly, I didn't feel all that bothered by this fact.

"Right back atcha," said Rod. "Looking forward to working with you, Commander."

"We'll probably cause you some trouble as we learn the ropes, but we'll try our hardest."

"We're in your care..."

The three princes didn't seem to mind Lorek's lack of formality either, forgoing any rebuke and instead addressing him respectfully as their leader.

I followed suit. "I look forward to working with you as well, Commander."

"Wow, everyone's so polite all of a sudden, ha ha. Let's give it our all, everyone." As Lorek laughed, Ralaire jumped up and down atop the commoner's head. She was simply adorable. "Let me introduce you to my vice-commander," Lorek continued. "Lambert, come here for a sec."

"Coming." A slender, academic-looking boy came at Lorek's call. I happened to recognize him.

"This is Lambert. Miss Claire might know him; he's Lene's older brother."

"We've met," I affirmed.

"Thank you for taking care of my sister," Lambert said, offering us the perfect bow. His mannerisms were so courteous; he felt more like a true commander than his superior.

"So you're a commoner, then?" Rod said. "Dang, you must be quite something to have been accepted into the Academy Knights despite that."

"No, no, not at all."

"C'mon now, Lambert," Lorek said. "No need for modesty, Master Rod's right. Your fighting ability may be average, but your intellectual gifts are unique."

"Oh? How so?" Yu asked, curious.

"He's an unparalleled genius when it comes to monsters, particularly with regard to making them familiars and otherwise controlling them."

"You don't say?" I cast my gaze toward the top of the commoner's head.

"Thanks for your help the other day, Lambert," a gentle voice said.

"Master Kristoff!"

A tall boy with blond hair and blue eyes appeared. He carried himself with grace and confidence that rivaled that of the three princes. I knew him to be Kristoff Achard, Catherine's half brother and heir to House Achard. He was also Loretta's fiancé.

"I'm glad you could make it, Commander."

"Please, Lorek. I'm not the commander anymore, nor even a member of the Academy Knights. I wouldn't even be allowed into this room if it weren't for your invitation." Kristoff gave us a wry grin. "But enough of that. Would you like to try one of these? They're a baked sweet known as a 'doughnut.'"

He pulled out a circular cake from a paper bag he held and handed it to Lorek. From the look on Lorek's face as he took a bite, it was evidently delectable.

"Sweets aside, what the heck are those two talking about?"

"What, indeed."

"Beats me..."

The three princes seemed stumped by this exchange, but I understood it.

Lorek seemed to pick up on their confusion. "Do you all remember how there were rumors of a monster in the vicinity of the academy last year?"

"Oh, I remember hearing something like that."

"Right, a monster used by the army escaped, or something like that."

"A chimera, from what I heard..."

As was to be expected of the princes, even though the event had nothing to do with them, they had kept tabs on all important happenings.

"So you did hear the rumors. Oh, would you like to try some doughnuts as well? They're surprisingly delicious," Kristoff offered.

"Don't see why not."

"Hey, these are pretty good."

"Not bad..."

The princes seemed to have favorable impressions of the pastries as well. Out of curiosity, I asked for one too, but I wasn't really a fan. The doughnut wasn't terrible, just a touch oily for me.

"Anyway, you were saying?" Rod said.

"Right. As you heard, there was a chimera in the area," Kristoff began, his voice soft. "The Academy Knights were able to locate and face it thanks to a citizen report, but...on account of a blunder on my part, a citizen was hurt in the process, and the chimera ultimately escaped."

"That wasn't your fault!" Lorek protested. "It was the fault of those noble-elitist students getting in the way when they tried to take the achievement for themselves!"

"That's right!" Lambert agreed. "I can't believe they had the nerve to blame y—"

"In the end," Kristoff interrupted, silencing them, "there's no changing the fact that someone got hurt. Marielle Monte, I believe her name was. I heard she had to close her sweets shop due to her heavy injuries." He looked deeply saddened by the event. "But Lambert later caught the escaped chimera with the magic tool he was working on."

"Thanks to that, I was able to join the Academy Knights despite being a commoner," said Lambert. "But Master Kristoff was ultimately obligated to resign."

"As commander, it was only right that I take responsibility and do so."

"But—"

"Let's leave it at that. We're before the princes."

"Right..."

I could tell Lambert had a great deal of respect for Kristoff. Unlike his father Clément, Kristoff treated people equally, regardless of status—something I'd heard made him popular with the common folk.

"Forgive me for my belated congratulations. Your Royal Highnesses, Miss Claire, and those of you whom I haven't yet had the pleasure of meeting: Congratulations on joining the Academy Knights. Please take good care of the organization." Kristoff gave us a short bow and left the room, likely out of consideration. It would sour the mood to have an ex-commander who had been forced to resign in disgrace lingering around—or so he likely assumed.

"Bit of a shame that a guy like him's not being put to use somewhere," said Rod.

"Yes, but there's his father to consider..." said Yu.

"I am unfond of Marquess Achard..." said Thane.

The princes seemed to hold a favorable impression of Kristoff, but the same couldn't be said for his father, Clément. They might've liked to put Kristoff to work for them, but doing so would inadvertently empower House Achard—and by extension, its arrogant family head, Clément.

"Mishh Cwaireee!"

"What, commoner? And don't talk with bread in your mouth. What if Ralaire picks up your bad habits?"

"You nobles have it rough, huh?"

"You're just now realizing? We're nothing like you happy-go-lucky commoners."

"I guess I was lucky to be born a commoner, then!" As I looked at her carefree face, I felt all the tension in my body fade. "Anyway, it's probably fine to just forget about House Achard. It's not like your father would let a talented guy like Kristoff go to waste, yeah?"

"I suppose."

The commoner seemed to ponder something at that moment. I didn't know it yet, but I would one day be very involved with both Kristoff and the chimera he had mentioned.

Our first job as Academy Knights was to check up on a recent rumor that had been spreading among the students.

"They say a ghost appears at night," the commoner told me one day.

A g-ghost? As shameful as it was to admit, I wasn't particularly...enthused about ghosts. An incident long ago had left me awfully frightened of all things supernatural. "I-I see. Right. A ghost. A *ghost*-ghost. Okay." I was terrified out of my wits, but I didn't let it show. If the commoner ever learned of my fears, I would never hear the end of it.

"Where did you see it?"

"My friend said she saw it in the stairwell between the second and third floors, but I saw it in the home ec classroom."

"So it's moving around. What did it look like?"

The commoner quickly proceeded to gather information. I, on the other hand, stood tense with fear, terrified by the thought that the ghost might appear at any moment. Even so, I couldn't shirk my duties. As a proud member of House François, I would see to my honorable duty as an Academy Knight.

"Well...I didn't recognize it as a ghost at first. I just thought it looked strange, but then I got closer and it splashed water on me."

"W-water?" I asked.

"Yes. It must be the ghost of a girl who drowned in the academy's river!"

"Eep!"

"What's wrong, Miss Claire?"

"I-It's nothing." I quickly downplayed my little shriek. I'd heard a rumor that a girl had passed away in that river, which was indeed most terrible, but why was she going out of her way to haunt the living merely because of that?! I wasn't particularly *afraid* of ghosts or anything—perish the thought. I simply wished for the boundary between this world and the next to be afforded a little more respect!

Really now... Who was I trying to convince with such a pathetic excuse?

"Thank you for the information."

"I'm counting on you! Please get rid of it!"

The commoner and I continued to consult with our classmates for some time. Three points consistently arose in these testimonies: the sightings took place at night, were always near the stairwell or in the home ec classroom, and water was somehow involved.

"Let's go check out the scenes of the sightings next."

"Can't you do that alone?"

"Why would I? Aren't two sets of eyes better than one?"

"I-I suppose..." I tried to discreetly worm my way out of going, but the stupid commoner didn't pick up on my desire. If I were with Lene, she'd have understood and offered to do it without me. Unfortunately, Lene was busy helping my father at the time.

We reached the home ec classroom soon enough. While it appeared normal on the surface, something about the place felt eerie to me.

"Here we are."

"Oh dear, it's locked. How unfortunate. I suppose we'll have to come back another time."

"No need, I borrowed the key."

"O-oh."

The commoner took out the key and turned the lock, opening it with a click. She then waltzed in with no fear, something I found unbelievable.

I peered in from the hallway. The cooking classroom seemed normal enough.

"Please look around the entrance, Miss Claire. I'll check out the back."

"You will not give me orders!"

"Okay then, do you want to look in the back?"

I paused. "No, I'll let you do it."

The idea of compromising with the commoner infuriated me, but scary things were scary. However, I had a job to do, so despite my trepidations, I began searching near the entrance. Things seemed ordinary enough—until I saw it.

"Eek! Commoner! You! *Rae!*" Having lost my composure, I inadvertently called the commoner by name, not that I had the wits to mind my faux pas.

"What's wrong?"

"Look! R-right there! Wait, why are you giggling?"

"Oh, sorry. You're just so precious."

"This is no time to play the fool! Look!" I pointed toward the doorway of the classroom, where a blue gel-like substance was stuck to the ground.

"What is this? Doesn't seem like your typical cooking mess."

I trembled in fear, but the commoner was fine and even reached out to touch the substance.

"Don't touch that! You don't even know what it is!"

"Oh my. Are you worried about me?"

"I just don't want to get caught up in any trouble you invite!" The rude truth slipped out of my mouth. But that was how I genuinely felt, so what did it matter?

"All right, I understand. We'll leave it for the research department." The commoner borrowed a pair of chopsticks and an empty jar from the classroom to collect the blue substance.

The research department she referred to was as its name implied: a department in the academy that handled academic investigations. They had originally focused on things related to natural sciences, but with the discovery of magic stones had come a paradigm shift. Now they studied all things arcane, like magic stones, monsters, and magic itself. Lene's brother Lambert studied monsters there as well.

"Doesn't look like there are any other clues here."

"Then let's hurry up and go."

"Right. Let's come back at night," the commoner said.

"Pardon...?" I couldn't believe my ears. This place was terrifying enough in the day, and she wanted us to come back after sundown?

"Once night comes, we might be able to spot the real culprit."

"B-but... What will we do if a ghost really does show up?"

"We'll just have to catch or exterminate it. Has anyone ever seen a real ghost before, anyway?"

"Yes, at least from what I've heard. One of my friend's friends apparently saw one, in fact."

"Ah... So the tradition of telling ghost stories exists over here too. Weird for a fantasy genre."

What nonsense was she prattling on about? "The only weird thing here is you. And aren't things like this best left to the military?"

"Unless it's a bona fide undead, the Academy Knights are strong enough to take care of a ghost. Actually, we don't even know if there's a ghost in the first place."

"P-perhaps, but we found that gel stuff, didn't we?"

"Don't you worry. Whatever happens, I'll protect you."

"Don't patronize me! I can protect myself!" I snapped, frustrated with the commoner's typical lackadaisical attitude.

Oh dear. I practically just agreed to return later this evening, I realized. It was too late for regrets, however.

"Sounds good. Back tonight it is!"

I sighed. "Why do you look like you're enjoying this so much?"

Night came. The academy dorm grew quiet as the time for lights-out drew near. We returned to the home ec classroom and carefully looked around.

"It's empty..."

"It certainly looks that way."

"Looks like coming back was a waste of time. All those ghost-sightings were no doubt figments of the imagination."

"Just in case, let's keep watch tonight."

"Here?!" I began to doubt the commoner's sanity. Why would

anyone want to stay overnight in a place where a ghost might appear? Surely she was joking.

"It's fine. I told Lene what we were up to, so she prepared bedding for us."

The lack of bedding wasn't my problem! More importantly... "You planned for this all along?"

"Yep." The commoner turned to me with a happy smile. I was livid. "I'll prepare the bedrolls for us."

"You don't seriously intend to spend the night here, do you?"

"But I do!" She began to prepare the bedrolls, but...

Hey, hey, hey!

"Okay, sleepy time," she said.

"You've only laid out one bedroll! There are two! Lay them both out!"

"Huh? But then I won't be able to sleep in the same bedroll as you, Miss Claire."

"Exactly!"

"You're so selfish."

"*I'm* selfish?! You can't be serious!"

How many times had we had these back-and-forths by now? She could be so insufferable at times, but I had to admit that my fear had subsided a bit, thanks to her antics.

"Go ahead and get in first," she said.

"And what are you going to do?"

"I thought I would make a midnight snack." The commoner donned an apron over her pajamas, then took ingredients out of the room's cold storage and measured them out.

"You can cook...?" I asked.

"Of course. I'm a commoner."

"Ah. Right."

There were some noble ladies who made sweets as a hobby, but I personally didn't cook at all. Somehow, I felt as if I had yet again lost to the commoner, and I didn't quite like it.

"I've been attempting new recipes lately. It's been pretty fun."

"Is that right? What a fitting pastime for a commoner," I spat. However, a question then came to mind. "Wait... But you spend all day serving at my side. Just when would you have time to cook?"

"I do it in the middle of the night when no one's looking."

"Oh, is that...so...?" My mind connected the dots. "In the middle of the night... Here in the home ec classroom?"

"Indeed."

"Does that mean... You're the ghost?"

"Most likely!"

"I'm going back to my room!" I declared. *How absurd! She must've known all along she was the cause of the rumors! What was all my worrying for?!*

Fed up, I jumped out of my bedroll and made for the exit. At that moment, a blue entity swept up in front of me.

"Eek! I-It's here!"

"Look again, Miss Claire. Say 'hi,' Ralaire."

"Huh?"

Indeed, now that I looked again, I realized that the blue entity was merely the commoner's familiar, Ralaire.

"Don't tell me, that gel-like substance from earlier..."

"Was from Ralaire, yep."

The bodies of water slimes were formless; if they brushed against something rough, a part of their bodies might scrape off. The truth rendered me speechless. I groaned, "You and your pet can be a real nuisance."

"I *am* sorry for not telling you. Please accept this as my apology." The commoner held out some kind of dark-brown baked sweet.

"What is this?"

"A brand-new sweet I came up with. I hope it's to your liking."

"Unlikely. Only something on the level of Broumet's sweets can suit...my...tastes..." Before I could finish my words, I found myself hooked by the sweet aroma wafting up from the plate. I took a bite, and a rich chocolate flavor filled every corner of my mouth. "Wha—it's delicious! What is this? It's like cake, but it's thick and creamy on the inside."

"It's called fondant au chocolat. It's chocolate cake with warm, melted chocolate inside."

"Chocolate is a novel new ingredient that even Broumet only recently acquired, so how do you know how to cook with it...? Who *are* you?" Come to think of it, there were a lot of mysteries surrounding the commoner. She had won over my father, made me promise strange things when she won her victories over me, and now here she was, knowing how to deftly cook with a delicacy no commoner could possibly know anything about. I sent her a sharp, suspicious glare.

"Why, I am nothing but a slave to your love, Miss Claire."

"Stop trying to sweep things under the rug with your jokes!"

"Come now. This sweet is best eaten hot, so eat up. I'll make some tea."

"Good grief... Nevertheless, this cake is divine. I offer my compliments."

"Thank you very much."

We had tea afterward. I indulged the commoner's nonsense for a bit, which soon put me to sleep.

"Heck yeah. This overnight date was a great success."

"Be quiet, commoner...zzz..."

I felt like the commoner said something inane as I drifted off, but I had long since passed into a chocolate-filled dream.

Sometime after the ghost incident, I was making my way back to the dorm with Lene and the commoner after classes.

"Oh? Isn't that girl over there part of your entourage, Miss Claire?" the commoner said.

"Don't call them that," I snapped. "But yes, that's Loretta, isn't it?"

"And that boy beside her appears to be Master Kristoff," Lene said.

Loretta and Kristoff were talking on a bench surrounded by flower beds off to the side of the pathway.

"Well, they *are* engaged. I'm sure they have a ton they'd like to discuss," the commoner said.

"We shouldn't interrupt their moment," Lene said.

THE CHEEKY MAID AND ME

"It doesn't look like they're having much of a moment to me..." I said. Their conversation didn't seem to be a pleasant one. Kristoff appeared to be speaking rather calmly, but Loretta was tense. Kristoff was nothing like his father, so I doubted he was saying anything cruel, but I couldn't help worrying.

I also couldn't very well barge in on their private time, as Lene said. So instead, I would simply have to walk past them.

"Oh! Miss Claire!"

"Oh my, if it isn't Miss Claire. Good day to you."

Then Loretta and Kristoff noticed and called out to me, so I gave in and walked over to their bench.

"Hello to you both. Might I inquire as to what you were discussing?" Without revealing the fact that I had just been observing them, I greeted them with a measured bow. Behind me, Lene and the commoner bowed as well.

"We were just considering whether we might have our ceremony soon, now that Loretta's turned sixteen," Kristoff said.

"Oh, I see! Congratulations, Loretta."

"Ah...well..." Loretta seemed uncertain.

Kristoff gave her a wry grin, then shrugged. "But it seems she still has some reservations about our marriage."

"Oh?"

"N-not at all, Master Kristoff!" Loretta said quickly. "I just haven't yet become a lady worthy of you. Please give me some more time to take homemaking lessons..."

Just what's going on here? I wondered.

Loretta's family, House Kugret, was affiliated with House

François's faction. As I mentioned before, House Kugret was known for its long line of military officers and had adopted the study of magic early, thus earning them a powerful voice in the kingdom's military affairs. Kristoff's father, Clément, was wary of their growth, however, which was why he'd paired his son with Loretta in a bid to weaken House François's strengthening influence over the army.

That said, the marriage proposal was by no means a bad deal for Loretta. She might have descended from a powerful military family line, but the one to inherit the family title and wealth would be Lorek, the eldest son. As a girl, she would eventually have to wed *some* noble—or at least she would have if not for her special circumstances. It was a small misfortune that she was being wed to House Achard, enemies of House François, but the Achard pedigree was some of the finest in Bauer. There could be no more commendable partner for her.

"I think you're fine as you are, Loretta," Kristoff said.

"Indeed. You're a wonderful lady," I followed up.

"Miss Claire..." For some reason, Loretta looked at me with the soulful eyes of an abandoned puppy.

"Ha ha, it looks like Loretta wants to stay by Miss Claire's side a little longer," he joked.

"M-Master Kristoff!"

"Huh?" I hadn't a clue what was going on.

"She's still more at ease being with her friends than me. I have no choice but to back down, given that she's clearly not ready to think about marriage," he said.

"Loretta…"

My friend hung her head bashfully.

"I have no qualms with waiting, but my father's been pestering me. I'm a little worried about what he might do if we postpone the ceremony too long," Kristoff said. Certainly, Clément was the type of man to seize by force whatever failed to come his way naturally. "I'll try to convince him, though. Can I count on you to be there for Loretta in case something happens, Miss Claire?" he asked, bowing his head.

"Please raise your head, Master Kristoff. Loretta's my friend. If your father attempts to make an untoward move against her, I'll face him as a member of House François."

"Thank you." Kristoff smiled, reassured.

"Wait," Loretta said.

"Loretta?"

"I'll do it. Let's go through with the ceremony." Though she said this, she seemed a bit sorrowful as she did. "In exchange, please hold it after the Autumn Concert."

"Oh, the annual performance?"

The Autumn Concert was hosted by the kingdom after the Harvest Festival. Talented musicians from all around the world were invited to play on its stage, and it was every musicians' dream to join them.

"Were you invited to play this year?" Kristoff asked.

"No… But I'm working my hardest to earn an invitation."

"I see."

Only the finest musicians were invited. Loretta was an

up-and-coming young star, but she had yet to be asked to perform at any Autumn Concerts thus far. Most of the invited musicians had a wealth of experience; the only one from our age group to receive that recognition was Thane.

"What if you don't get invited?" Kristoff asked.

"Then you can go ahead and immediately prepare the ceremony. I don't want to keep you waiting any longer than I must."

The participants for the Autumn Concert were set in stone by summer every year. In other words, if Loretta didn't receive an invitation by summer, there would be no use waiting any longer.

"Very well, I'll wait. I was planning to wait however long you needed in the first place, so long as you agreed to marry me. Nothing could make me happier."

"Thank you."

Something felt off about this conversation. As I noted earlier, this marriage benefited them both. And yet...

"This kind of feels like one of those forced marriages, huh?" the commoner blurted out the very thing I had tactfully avoided saying.

"Commoner!" I exclaimed, appalled.

"What? Am I wrong? Marriage should be a happy thing, but it's like these two are only begrudgingly getting—"

"*Enough.* Not another word out of you."

"Okaaaay." Reluctantly the commoner held her tongue.

Nevertheless, her words rang true to me.

"Your name is Rae, isn't it?" Kristoff said. "You may not be far off the mark."

"Master Kristoff?!" Loretta exclaimed.

"Unlike commoners, nobles marry for political reasons," he continued. "Our families come before our own feelings. Many who marry do so without truly desiring the union."

Loretta hung her head.

"Even so, I love Loretta. I wish to make her happy. The question is whether she feels the same way."

Loretta looked at him with a start, a bit guiltily so.

"Loretta," said Kristoff, "I know someone else has taken your heart, and I can't force you to love me. I may love you, but your feelings are your own to do with what you will, as sad as that may make me."

"Master Kristoff..."

"So there's no need to rush our marriage. I want you to be happy, even if I can't be the one to make you so."

I couldn't believe my ears. Kristoff was basically saying she could annul their engagement if she desired.

"Master Kristoff?"

"Think carefully on your feelings, Loretta. We can continue this conversation once you have. I'm sorry for trying to hurry things along." With that, Kristoff bowed and left.

"Loretta..."

"I'm sorry, Miss Claire. I need some time to think. Could you leave me to myself for a while?"

"Of course..." I tried to offer words of comfort to Loretta but was gently turned away. Left with no other choice, I made to leave with Lene and the commoner.

"You nobles have it rough, huh?"

"Haven't I told you before? We're nothing like you happy-go-lucky commoners."

"Oh, I'm sure. Still, I'm surprised you haven't caught on..."

"Hm? What do you mean?"

"Indeed, whatever do I mean?"

"Rae!" Lene warned. It seemed she understood what the commoner was hinting at.

"What's going on, Lene?"

"I'm sorry, Miss Claire. It is not something I can say."

"Even if I order you to?"

"My apologies. This is something you must realize yourself."

Lene never budged when she got like this. But she was loyal, and she never did anything I wouldn't want, so I had no option but to believe she knew best and trust her.

"...And that's what happened today."

"Uh-huh. I see, I see," Catherine said with a sleepy drawl. With the lights out in our room, she laid in the bunk bed above mine, listening.

"So? What do you think they're hiding from me?"

"Claire, you're...just so Claire, aren't you?" It seemed that somehow, Catherine had figured out what I couldn't, despite only having a secondhand account to go off of.

"Oh, not you too. Won't somebody just tell me already? Jeez!"

"I'm sorry, but Lene's right. This is something you have to realize yourself. Nighty night."

"Hey, wait, Catherine!"

But soon I heard her begin to snore.

Just what is going on...?

I went to sleep confused that night. It wouldn't be until quite a bit later that I finally understood.

"The Foundation Day Festival?" the commoner asked.

"That's right," Lorek answered.

The Academy Knights had gathered in our usual meeting room, having been summoned by Lorek to discuss the yearly celebration of the Royal Academy's founding, the Foundation Day Festival. Guests were allowed to visit on the day of the festival, so it was a good chance to show off the school. That being said, more than anything, the festival was a chance for students to let loose; showcasing the academy to outsiders was really just an excuse to have fun. Every class was to prepare an attraction or exhibition of some kind, which consequently meant we Academy Knights would soon be very, very busy.

"We'll have much to do as the festival approaches—approving class requests for goods, loaning out equipment, you get the idea. I'll be assigning everyone tasks. If you're not quite sure what you need to do, please ask," Lorek said.

"Yo, Commander. The Academy Knights are going to prepare something for the festival too, right?" Rod asked as he sat askew in his chair—rather rudely as well.

"That's right. Normally, we set up a café."

"Sounds boring. Let's do something more unique." Rod grinned wickedly, the wheels in his mind obviously turning.

"What do you have in mind, Brother?" Yu inquired, interested.

"Isn't a normal café fine...?" Thane said, unenthusiastic. He wasn't too fond of these kinds of frivolous events.

"Cross-dressing cafés have become pretty popular in the capital lately. How about we do that?" Rod offered.

Misha balked at the term. "What is a cross-dressing café?"

"It's your typical café, just with the waitstaff boys dressing as girls and vice versa. All we do is switch clothes—but that alone would make it a lot more interesting than normal, don't you think?" Rod smiled proudly.

"Master Rod, you are aware that means you'll have to dress as a girl, right? Is that...permitted of royalty?" I asked. It was an unwritten rule that the royal family should model behavior by which the citizens of the kingdom would live their own lives.

"We just have to make sure we don't get caught," he said, cackling with a mischievous smile.

Why were boys all so *childish*? Or was it just Rod who never seemed to grow up?

"Girls dressing as boys is odd enough, but I'd rather not have to see boys dress as girls. Although..." I looked around at the line-up of boys before us. All three of the princes had a particular beauty, what with their fair faces. "I take it back. This could work."

"Uh, the rest of us guys get a say in this too, right? Because it's a hard no from me. C'mon, you're with me on this, right,

Lam...bert...?" Lorek began to complain just as I had, but he slowly trailed off and froze as he took in the sight of Lambert beside him. While not as much as the princes, Lambert also possessed an effeminate charm that could very well be complemented by girls' clothes. "Oh, I see how it is," Lorek continued, trembling. "So the only laughingstock here's going to be me."

Lorek wasn't unattractive by any means; he was a handsome noble in his own right. Unfortunately, his looks were the rugged, manly sort—a poor match for feminine garb.

"So, no objections?" Rod wrapped things up, ignoring Lorek's distress. It was very much like him to force things along like this. Poor commander.

"It's fine by me," Yu said.

"If this is what everyone wants..." Thane half-heartedly echoed.

"I have no objections," Misha agreed.

"It's fine with m—"

"Miss Claire in boys' clothes...eh heh heh heh..."

"I've changed my mind. One vote against." I was about to give my approval but swiftly reversed course upon hearing the commoner giggling. Nevertheless, my one vote meant nothing against the majority.

"Um, I also object..." Lorek said.

"I'm pretty sure this is out of our hands already, Commander," Lambert said, putting a hand on Lorek's shoulder.

"It's decided, then. This year, the Academy Knights will host a cross-dressing café called Cavalier," Rod said.

"Cavalier?" the commoner said, unfamiliar with the word.

"It's the official name of the Academy Knights. 'Cavalier' means knight," Lambert answered. The name wasn't used for the knights much anymore. It was honestly impressive that Rod knew it at all.

"Doesn't 'cavalier' also mean 'aloof elegance'?" the commoner asked.

"Yes, but that wording comes off as a bit crude. I'd prefer to describe it as *'unaffected* elegance.'"

I was of the same mind as Lambert. How you worded something greatly changed the impression it left. Such was the fundamental basis of poetry. But I couldn't very well expect a commoner to be familiar with such things, now could I?

"That description fits Miss Claire to a tee! She's such a cavalier girl...cavalier... Miss Claire's a *cabaret* girl!" The commoner was speaking nonsense yet again. I hadn't a clue what a cabaret girl was supposed to be, but I could tell it wasn't to be taken as a compliment, given the amused look on her face.

I would later learn that a cabaret girl was a type of *lady of the night*—although not one whose work included sexual companionship but rather a more chaste intimacy. I scolded the commoner fiercely when I learned of this, not because she had teased me by associating me with that trade but because she had meant the term in the derogatory sense.

It seemed the commoner hadn't known at the time, but there were women in the Bauer Kingdom who made their living in similar ways. There were those who looked down on them for their profession, but it was a simple fact of the matter that many noblemen made use of their services. These ladies had to be expert communicators to do their work. Unlike most commoners, they stayed up-to-date on current events by reading newspapers, all so they could discuss the latest news with clients. They furthermore worked hard to maintain favorable looks and trained in fine arts such as music to better entertain those who bought their time. Even the most fundamental aspect of their trade, simple conversation, was polished to perfection.

Of course, I didn't think for a moment that all those who worked in this field did so by choice rather than circumstance, but it was absurd to insult such hard-working women.

But I digress. In this particular moment, I had no idea what a cabaret girl was supposed to be. "I have no idea what you're talking about, but I get the impression that isn't a compliment."

"It *is* a compliment! If you were a cabaret girl, I'd go spend big bucks to be with you every day!"

"Once again, just what on earth are you talking about?!"

Like always, the commoner was teasing me.

"Let's try putting your hair in an updo!" she said.

"An updo...? Whatever do you mean by that?"

"It's a special hairstyle only permitted for cabaret girls!"

I'd later find out this hairstyle she referred to as an "updo" was a fashionable hairstyle often associated with cabaret girls that was painstakingly devised by women from the commoner's world. Apparently, it was fairly difficult to pull off and required a visit to a hairdresser to set every time, all paid out of pocket.

"Oh? Special, you say? H-hmph! I'll make an exception and allow it!" I hadn't a clue what this updo would look like, but I was curious as to what made it special.

The meeting came to an end, so we left and met up with Lene, who had returned to my room ahead of us. Catherine had made herself invisible again.

"What are you doing, Rae?" Lene asked.

"I'm about to turn Miss Claire into a cabaret girl."

"A what?"

"All right, Miss Claire. Ready?"

I sat down before the dresser, and the commoner got to work changing my hairstyle.

"Oooh, is that what it's supposed to look like?" Lene said.

"Mm-hmm. You make a foundation with half of the hair in the back and hold it in place with bobby pins," the commoner said.

I couldn't see what was going on from my seat, but it seemed the commoner had some hairdressing skill, considering the lack of painful tugging.

"It's a good thing your hair is already curled nicely. It's the curling that takes the most time."

"I have Lene to thank for that."

"Much obliged."

Apparently my regular hairstyle was a good base for this updo thing. It didn't take even thirty minutes for the commoner to finish. "Done!"

"Wow! Miss Claire, it looks wonderful."

"Uh-huh... Not bad," I said, turning my head left and right to check. This was the first time I'd seen such a flashy hairstyle in the kingdom.

"You look amazing, Miss Claire! You look *just like* a cabaret girl, through and through!"

"I-I do?"

I should've known she was teasing me by that point. Unfortunately, I wouldn't realize it until much later.

"Miss Claire, do you want to keep this hairstyle for a bit?" Lene suggested with a smile. I understood why. In her own way, she was suggesting I move on. But...

"No... My normal hairstyle is fine. Can you change it back, Lene?" I couldn't relinquish it just yet. My usual hairstyle was the same as my late mother's. It was what connected me to her.

"Of course," she said, sounding slightly disappointed. She had probably hoped I could overcome my lingering grief. But I didn't have it in me to do so yet.

"But I love that about you too!" the commoner suddenly blurted. Nonsense, again.

"What are you going on about?"

"Sorry, my love overflowed a bit."

"Whatever. Just return to your room."

To my surprise, the commoner obeyed and turned to leave. She paused, however, and called out my name. "Oh, Miss Claire?"

"What?"

"I can't wait to see you dressed like a boy!"

"Hurry up and get out!"

Of course she would leave while prattling more nonsense. Goodness...

"Why don't we try this, then...?"

"Hmm, I think paper would still serve better there..."

After classes, I returned to the Academy Knight room like always and found a seldom-seen pair there.

"Why, it's not often I see you two together. What are you working on?"

"Oh, hello, Miss Claire. We're just putting together something my family requested," Pepi answered.

Lambert silently bowed.

"Your family was House Barlier, right?" mused the commoner, who had accompanied me.

"Hmph, a commoner like you shouldn't speak my family name so flippantly!" Pepi snapped. Her distaste for the commoner was understandable, given how the girl always treated my friends more like my tag-alongs. Pepi pinned the commoner with a fierce glare, but the commoner seemed unfazed.

"And your father was...Master Patrice, correct?" the commoner continued.

"Wh-what the... Keep my father's name out of your—"

"He's a seemingly unreliable man who turns surprisingly firm when cornered. If he sets his mind to it, he can flip any situation on its head and beat the odds. He's got a fair cult following."

"You understand well!" Pepi proudly shook hands with the commoner, who had, somehow, eloquently summarized the personality of Baron Patrice—someone she couldn't possibly have met before.

Pepi, are you really that easy to please? I wearily thought to myself.

Meanwhile, Ralaire trembled atop the commoner's head, perhaps surprised by the speed of Pepi's change of heart.

"You love your father, don't you, Miss Pepi?" the commoner asked.

"Of course I do! He's the best father in the world!"

"Bit of a daddy's girl, huh?"

"I am! Wait, what's that mean exactly?"

"Oh, don't worry about it."

The topic of their conversation aside, Pepi was clearly more open to the commoner now. Perhaps praising her father was the secret to getting on her good side.

"Hello, Miss Claire, Rae. Has my sister been serving you well?" Lambert asked.

"Hello, Lambert. Lene's been wonderful to me, unlike this commoner here," I replied.

"Eh heh heh, you flatter me."

"That was *not* flattery!"

"Aha ha ha. I see you two get along." Lambert smiled the same soft smile I often saw on his sister's face. "Please continue to treat Lene well. She can be a bit of a handful whenever her switch gets flipped, but she's a good girl at heart."

"Yes, I'm well aware. What were you discussing with Pepi just now?"

"Oh, that? Pepi wanted to know if there were any magic tools that could make clerical work more efficient." Despite his young age, Lambert was one of the leading researchers of the magic tool research department and was frequently asked such questions because of it.

"Clerical work uses lots of paper, right?" Pepi elaborated. "But paper is pricey and bulky to store, so I was thinking maybe we could cut costs somewhere, or maybe even use something else entirely."

She had a fair point. Drafting documents was a big part of clerical work, but the cost of paper was a significant burden. Finding an alternative would be quite the innovation.

"And? Was there anything?" the commoner asked, to my surprise. Usually she flat-out ignored anything Pepi said.

"How unusual of you, commoner. You're listening to Pepi for once," I said.

"Yeah, well, I've had to deal with all that 'going paperless' jazz at work myself before, so—er, I mean—" She coughed. "Nothing..."

"Huh?" The commoner was babbling nonsense again. In other words, business as usual.

"I'm not sure what the commoner's on about, but Lambert's been telling me there's not much that can be done," Pepi said.

"Paper's simply too useful," Lambert went on. "It's thin and lightweight but still sturdy, and in the long history of information-storing media, it remains unmatched. Coming up with a replacement would be nigh impossible."

"I thought I was on to something though..." Pepi said sadly.

"It was a wonderful idea, Miss Pepi," he comforted.

"Do you often think about these kinds of things?" I asked.

"Huh? Oh, uh, I suppose? I'll have to marry into another house one day as I can't inherit, since I'm a girl, but my family's been generous enough to let me live freely, so I want to pay them back somehow before I'm wed."

"That's very admirable of you, Pepi," I said. From what I'd seen, not many nobles shared that mindset these days. Far from it, there were many who demonstrated no appreciation for their family at all and instead drove them to ruin through self-indulgence. I had to wonder, just where was their pride as the nobility of Bauer?

"Not at all. I'm only doing what's right, Miss Claire." Pepi smiled at my praise.

"Oh hey, I just realized, but Miss Loretta isn't with you today, is she?" the commoner said, sounding as though she really had only just noticed.

"You don't think we spend every waking moment together or something, do you...?" Pepi asked.

The commoner balked, eyes wide. "You don't?"

"M-Miss Claire..." Pepi turned to me, teary eyed.

"Don't waste your breath on her, Pepi. She'll only give you more headache."

Pepi sniffed. "Noted..."

I patted Pepi's head to comfort her.

"Hey, no fair! I want head pats too!" the commoner protested.

"You be quiet!"

"Ha ha ha..." Lambert laughed dryly. He was a commoner as well, so how had he ended up so different?

"Loretta has piano lessons," Pepi said. "You know, because the Foundation Day Festival is coming up."

"Ah, I see..."

"Hm? What's that got to do with anything?"

I understood at once, but the commoner didn't seem to. Even Ralaire expressed confusion, in her own way.

"Loretta will be performing at the Foundation Day Festival," I said.

"Not that you'd be able to understand how amazing that is!" Pepi scoffed.

"Uh-huh, is that so?" The commoner lost interest immediately. I had to wonder just how she could be so single-minded in her concerns. "Anyway, returning to what we were discussing earlier..."

"Which was?" I asked.

"That clerical efficiency stuff."

"What about it?"

"Well, isn't there a magic tool that records sound? With its small size and large storage size, it could be useful somehow."

"Huh? I've never heard of such a magic tool," I said.

"Me neither," Pepi said. "Does that even really exist? Tell us everything you know about it, commoner."

"Uh...sorry, but that was everything."

"I see..." Pepi's shoulders drooped.

"I know of it," Lambert said. "It's a very rare magic tool, so it's no surprise you haven't heard of it." He explained that while they did exist, only people like King l'Ausseil, Salas, or high-standing nobles like my father had access to them.

"Wait, then how do you, a commoner, know of such an item?!" I demanded.

"Who's to say? Perhaps I just so happened to overhear something about it somewhere."

"Is that right..."

The commoner was as shrouded in mystery as ever.

"Anyway, what do you think, Lambert? Would such a magic tool be useful?" she asked.

"I doubt it. Currently, only the best of the best artificers can make something like that. We're far from being able to mass produce it, meaning it'd be too expensive to use for something like clerical work."

"Gotcha. No good, then."

"I heard there were low-quality counterfeits secretly floating around, but that's probably nothing more than a rumor. Not even the Nur Empire with all its magic advancements can make them easily."

"Is that so?" The commoner seemed to have already lost interest again.

"Lambert?" Pepi asked with some curiosity.

"Yes?"

"Can I ask you to compile all the information you can on that magic tool and submit it to my father? There's potential here."

"I don't mind. I'll have it done in a day or two."

"Thank you."

It was hard to place too much blind faith in the words of two commoners, but it seemed Pepi saw potential nevertheless.

"On another note, shouldn't you be worried about someone leaking information, Lambert? It's odd that a commoner like this one knew of that magic tool," I said, gesturing toward my maid.

"You're right... I'll make sure to warn those involved." After Lambert said that, he took his leave.

"I think I'll head out as well, then," Pepi said.

"Please, stay if you'd like. This room isn't strictly forbidden to those not in the knights or anything," I said.

"I'm aware, but I have a violin lesson coming up soon."

"Ah, I see. Keeping up with Loretta, are we?"

"Yes!"

But of course she would be. Pepi's dream was to play on the same stage as her friend, after all.

"I bid you good day then, Miss Claire, and...you too."

"Good day, Pepi."

"Good day, Miss Pepi."

Pepi then left the room as well.

"Commoner, I take it you're done belittling Pepi?"

"Eh, I guess."

"Loretta and Pepi are my dear friends. Think of any disrespect shown to them as disrespect shown to me."

"I see... In other words, they're something like my rivals in love?"

"How did you even come to that conclusion?!"

After that, the three princes and the other Academy Knights trickled in, and my conversation with the commoner was put on indefinite hold. Looking back on it now, I had probably already realized by then that the commoner's expansive knowledge was far too unnatural to write off, but yet again, I willingly chose to turn a blind eye to reality.

"This is Lene, here to give us a lecture on service."

"Thank you for having me."

With only a few days left until the Foundation Day Festival, Lene was invited into the Academy Knight room and introduced by the commoner—all without anyone notifying me beforehand.

"What do you think you're doing, using my servant without my permission, commoner?" I said. Lene and the commoner seemed to get along well, but at the end of the day, Lene was *my* servant. I wouldn't stand for someone using her without my permission.

"Oh, sorry, I requested her," Rod said. Apparently he had been looking for someone to teach customer service and cooking to the Academy Knights for the cross-dressing café we'd be operating during the upcoming festival. That was when the commoner had overstepped her bounds and offered to introduce him to Lene. As I've noted, Lene's employer was my father and, by extension, myself. The proper thing to do for such a request would have been to go through me.

"In that case, that's fine." I backed down for the time being, however. I couldn't exactly complain to Rod, so instead I would scold the commoner later.

"We're all yours, Lene," the commoner said.

"Thank you, Rae. But I have one request before I begin instruction."

"Hmm? And what's that?" Yu asked.

"Unlike most of you, I am a commoner. I understand there are some commoners in the Academy Knights, but they are still among the elite and have passed a rigorous selection test. I'm sure many of you aren't pleased to be learning from someone like me."

Lene had a point. While it would be fine for the commoners, many nobles were highly conscious of their status and wouldn't take kindly to being taught by a commoner. I was fine with it, as I trusted her, but the others—particularly the princes—would likely have some reservations.

"So…?" Thane prompted. He likely didn't mean it, but with that perpetual stone face of his, he could come off as a bit intimidating. Not that Lene seemed to mind.

"I know it's bold of me to ask this, but I would like to request that when I am teaching, we disregard all distinctions between royalty, nobility, and commoner. You cannot serve customers if you cleave to such particularities."

"Fine by me. You guys have no problem with it either, right?" Rod said. Thane and Yu didn't seem to object either.

I was surprised they were so willing. Or maybe their status was just so many worlds removed from ours that being taught by a commoner didn't even register as an offense to them. At any rate, I was relieved Lene wouldn't be punished for her impertinence and so could breathe a sigh of relief. That was, until Lene said the most *outrageous* thing.

"Thank you very much. Starting now, and until the Foundation Day Fair, please call me Ms. Lene."

It was unthinkable enough for a commoner to instruct nobility and royalty, and now she wanted to be treated like a teacher? I was certain she had angered the princes, so I swept in to scold her. "Lene, don't get too haughty—"

"Ms. Lene, please," she interrupted.

"Wh-wh..." I stammered. *Y-you fool! Just be quiet and let me scold you!*

"Miss Claire, please address me correctly. Go ahead."

"Y-you..."

"Ha ha! She's funny. Claire, do it," Rod said.

He was laughing... Maybe this could actually work out? My heart raced as I pretended to obediently comply with Lene's demand. I could bear the humiliation if it would keep her safe. "Argh... Ms....Lene..."

"Louder, please."

Aren't you getting a little carried away?! I thought as my annoyance began to show. "Why you..."

"Heh heh. Claire, you gotta say it," Yu teased.

"Ms. Lene..." I relented.

"Very good, Miss Claire. Please address me in that way from now on."

"Oh, I'll get you for this later..." I muttered under my breath. Nevertheless, I was glad it didn't seem like Lene would be punished for her rudeness.

"So, what are you teaching us first, Ms. Lene?" Misha said, switching to her new term of address with no trouble at all. Misha was never the type to care much about status and was in fact a commoner like Lene herself these days. She probably had no reservations about this arrangement.

"First I'll be teaching you all how to mentally prepare yourself. Now what mindset do you think one must have in order to follow the Way of the Maid?"

"Th-the Way of the Maid?" I repeated, unnerved by the phrase.

Lene looked as if she were in a trance; I'd never seen her like this before. "Yes. That is what I'm here to teach you." Her smile was soft, but something about her was...*off*. To be blunt, she was terrifying. I could see Ralaire trembling atop the commoner's head. "There is great depth to this discipline. Under normal circumstances, it would be impossible to master it in a mere week."

I started, "Ah, none of us have any need to *master* this Way of the Maid—"

"However!" Lene interrupted, her voice growing ever more impassioned. "It is my wish to share the spirit of dedication and service with all of you, representatives of nobles and commoners alike as you are. For that reason alone, I stand before you today."

I felt like I could see something wicked looming behind Lene—an evil spirit, perhaps, that had suddenly possessed her.

"Ah, yes... The spirit of dedication and service is the essence of the Way of the Maid. You are likely as yet unfamiliar with the concept, but know that it is important and that it brings peace to our world."

As Lene's claims grew increasingly grandiose, I was helpless to stop her.

Lene's lecture lasted over an hour, and what an absolute honor it had been to take part in it... I did feel like something about me was somehow...off? But I simply couldn't identify what.

"With this, I believe you're all on your way to understanding the basics of the Way of the Maid."

"Yes, Ms. Lene."

"A very good response, Miss Claire. Let's review. What is the essence of the Way of the Maid?"

"Dedication and service, Ms. Lene."

"That's right. Well done."

"Thank you very much, Ms. Lene."

Indeed, dedication and service were two wonderful concepts that were closely tied to world peace. How could I have been so confused by such a simple truth earlier?

"Now, Master Rod. Where do the basics of the Way of the Maid begin?"

"With a greeting, Ms. Lene."

"Good. Let's try one all together, then."

"Welcome home, master!" everyone called out.

"I can't hear you!"

"Welcome home, master!" everyone shouted again.

"Good. I think you're starting to get it. Your teacher is very happy."

I was happy in turn to receive her praise.

"Um, Lene?" the commoner said nervously.

"*Ms.* Lene," Ms. Lene firmly corrected.

"Ms. Lene, isn't this lesson a bit...strange?"

"No, not at all. I just want everyone to understand the beauty of the Way of the Maid."

"I-I see..."

"Now you, Rae. 'Welcome home, master.'"

"W-welcome home...master."

It seemed the commoner was finally seeing the light. *Yes, let us all learn the Way of the Maid as one!*

"What are the basics of the Way of the Maid?" Ms. Lene asked.

"Devotion and service!" we answered.

"And how do you greet those you serve?"

"Welcome home, master!" we shouted.

In hindsight, it was very clear that there was something wrong with us.

"That was terrifying..." I said once I'd come to my senses a bit after leaving the Academy Knight room. *Devotion? Service? Oh please.* By the time I returned to my room, I was exhausted.

"My apologies. I got a little carried away." Lene smiled sweetly. It was hard to imagine she had been so terrifying mere moments before. Even now, I was still a little afraid of her and her border-line insane passion.

Ralaire, atop the commoner's head, didn't seem so chipper either. I'd wondered for a while now, but was it possible that Ralaire understood human speech?

"I don't even have the energy to be angry... I was surprised to see this side of you, Lene. I didn't know you had it in you."

"It's not a side I get the opportunity to exercise often."

"And it's not a side I'd ever like to see again..."

I felt like all I knew about Lene had been flipped on its head. Out of energy, I flopped onto my bed.

"You can't sleep yet, Miss Claire. You need to take a bath and change first."

"I'm tired. Just let me go to sleep..."

"No. Please get up."

"Ugh..."

"Get up."

"Yes, Ms. Lene! ...Ah." I shot up and responded by sheer reflex.

As I trembled with embarrassment, the commoner said, "It seems there were some unforeseen side effects to Lene's lecture..."

"More like unforeseen trauma!" I corrected her. This was all just too much.

"I wish I could forget all that happened today," I complained to Catherine after my maids left.

"Aww, don't say that."

I didn't know it yet, but in time I would come to treasure even these "traumatic" memories.

I was too nervous to sleep with the Foundation Day Festival only one day away. So instead, I chatted through the night with Catherine as we lay in our bunk beds, hers above mine. Eventually, we ran out of things to talk about and our conversation came to a halt. The whole academy was sound asleep at that point; the only thing I could hear was the sound of the candy being rolled around Catherine's mouth.

"Hey, Catherine. Could you—"

"Nooope."

"You don't even know what I was going to ask."

"I don't need to know. You're so tense, I can tell it's going to be a pain."

"Oh please. It's just a small request. Really."

"Uh-huh..." she said, unconvinced. I heard her slowly shift around in her upper bunk, then saw her hang over the edge to look at me. "Well, I suppose I could at least hear out my dear little Claire."

"You're too kind. Anyway, there's going to be a recital at tomorrow's festival, and I was wondering if you could come with me."

"Mmm...naaaah."

"Wha—Caterine!" She pulled herself back up and resumed a sleeping position. I got up and climbed the ladder to her bed.

"This recital is very important to my friend. It'll decide whether Loretta gets invited to the big Autumn Concert."

"Oooh. Yeah, that does sound important. But what's that got to do with me going?"

"Well... It's such an important recital that I'm afraid to go alone."

Loretta wasn't the type to buckle under pressure, but she wasn't beyond making mistakes either. If she didn't get an invitation to the Autumn Concert with tomorrow's performance, she would have to begin preparing for marriage like she'd promised. Kristoff probably wouldn't force her to keep her vow, but knowing Loretta's personality, she would see it through regardless. I was in favor of their marriage myself, but I also understood that Loretta wasn't ready for it yet. I therefore much preferred the idea of seeing her continue the path of music until she was.

"Don't you have somebody else you could invite? Like Lene?" Catherine asked.

"She'll be busy overseeing Cavalier all day."

"What about that commoner?"

"Her shift at Cavalier overlaps with Loretta's performance. And inviting her would only give me more to worry about in the first place!"

"Sheesh. So picky."

Wha—am I the problem here? I thought.

"Why don't you invite Master Thane?"

"What...?"

"The fine arts make a perfect date for royalty and nobles alike, right?"

"D-d-d-d-don't be silly! Why would Master Thane ever agree to go on a date with me?!"

However, I couldn't stop my wicked mind from imagining it...

"How beautiful..."
"Indeed, Loretta's performance was magnificent."
"No... I'm talking about you, Claire."
"Huh? M-Master Thane...?"
"The sweet melody of your voice is irresistible."
"Y-you jest..."
"Do I look like the kind of man who'd speak in jest?"
"Oh..."
"Look into my eyes, Claire."
"Master Thane..."
Then the two of us would lean in for a—

"Hello? Earth to Claire?"

"Whoa?!" I was brought back to my senses right before imagining the unthinkable. "A-anyway, I'm not asking Master Thane to the recital!"

"So *picky.*"

This is hardly being picky! I thought.

"What about Pepi, then?" she suggested.

"She's helping with her class's thing."

"Master Dole?"

"Work."

"Mmm..." Catherine pondered this for a short while. "Erm, Claire?"

"Yes?"

"Do you perhaps...not have friends?"

"D-don't be silly, socializing with other nobles is one of my many pastimes! I have a wealth of friends!"

"But then isn't it weird that you're so hard-pressed for someone to invite?"

"Th-that's..." I had no words to argue with. She'd hit the nail on the head.

"Besides, I'm missing a whole leg, y'know? It's tough for me to get around."

"Oh, I've got something for that. One moment." I unfolded the object I had stashed away in a corner of the room and placed it before the beds. "The commoner gave me the idea for this."

"What is it?"

"It's called a 'wheelchair,' apparently. It should be a lot faster than walking with a cane."

The commoner had suggested this device when I told her about Catherine's leg. Of course, she had only given me the idea. The actual creation of the wheelchair had been handled by a smith I commissioned.

"It seems it typically uses wheels, but Lambert had the idea to install wind-attribute magic stones to make it levitate slightly instead."

Stairs would have been difficult to handle with wheels, but most steps would be traversable with levitation. Even Levitation would have its limits, admittedly; the chair couldn't scale a steep cliff, for example. Wheels were also still attached for when the device ran out of magic, another of Lambert's suggestions. He had been very on board with the whole planning process, seeming to enjoy it as a thought experiment. He believed there would be great demand for the wheelchair among elderly nobles who could no longer walk.

"What do you think, Catherine? Will you come to the recital with me?"

For once, Catherine's ever sleepy eyes were open in surprise. She stared at the wheelchair and started to laugh. "Ha ha..."

"Hm?"

"Ha ha...ha ha ha!"

"Catherine?" I had never seen her like this before. She often put on a smile, but seeing her laugh from the bottom of her heart was a first. "I-Is something wrong?"

"Claire...are you stupid?"

"What?! Who do you think you're calling stupid?!" I said, indignant. However, I soon found myself speechless.

"I mean...why else would anyone go so far for a broken girl?"

"Oh, Catherine..." I saw tears well up in her eyes. Just how awful was her home life? Damn that Clément...

"I'll go," said Catherine.

"Huh?"

"Tomorrow's recital. I'll go. Please take me with you."

"Catherine!" Overjoyed, I climbed onto her bed and hugged her.

"Claaaire, you're hurting me!"

"Oh, sorry. But I'm grateful to hear you'll come."

"Thanks for the invitation. Anyway, how much did the wheelchair—"

"Don't you worry about that. It was but a paltry sum to me."

"But—"

"Please, accept it as a token of my friendship?"

Catherine hesitated. "Fine. Sheesh, there's no arguing with you, Claire."

"Hee hee." I went to bed feeling like I was on cloud nine, having secured a promise to go to the recital with Catherine. It would be our first outing together in ages. "I'm looking forward to tomorrow."

"Me too."

Catherine, sitting beside me in the wheelchair I'd given her, exclaimed in awe at the sight before us. "Whoa... This place is incredible."

Her reaction was only natural.

Today was the day of the long-awaited Foundation Day Festival. Various functions were being held within the academy itself, but the recital was in the Royal Academy concert hall, located right on campus grounds. I had just barely made it in time to come with Catherine after finishing my shift at Cavalier.

The concert hall had five auditoriums of different sizes which spanned about a fourth of the area of the academy in total.

Having been established by the royal family, its furnishings were of the highest quality and were changed out every few decades to give the place a fresh look while retaining its historic air.

Catherine and I oohed and aahed at the elegant relief sculpted over the entrance for a moment, then proceeded into the large auditorium.

"You'll have a hard time finding a better concert hall. It's even more impressive than the Nur Empire's Imperial Theater or Sousse's Royal Opera House."

"I believe it. This interior has to be on par with the royal palace." Catherine eyed her surroundings curiously, as though it were all alien to her. Despite coming from a high-standing noble family, she had little experience with high society because of her father.

I had claimed to be too scared to come alone to such an important event in order to get her to come with me, but that wasn't the whole truth. I had also wanted to get Catherine out of that cramped room. While all other nobles did as we liked in our free time, Catherine only ever stayed in her room. Occasionally she went outside, but with her leg, she couldn't go far. Moreover, with her father being who he was, she didn't have any friends other than myself.

"Aren't you glad you came after all, Catherine?"

"Yeah. Thank you, Claire."

I smiled, and she smiled back. I was truly happy I'd invited her out, but...

"Ladies, I ask that you not get too carried away. My master wishes Lady Catherine to maintain a low profile."

Here to throw a damper on our fun was a tall, brown-eyed, black-haired, older woman. Her black hair was pulled into a tight bun, giving her a strict appearance. She was Catherine's maid.

"Sorry, Emma. But just look at this building! Doesn't it make you the least bit excited?" Catherine asked.

"Not particularly. I am more concerned as to how you may be attracting undue and undesirable attention." Without so much as a twinge in her expression, Emma looked down at Catherine's wheelchair.

Emma's fears weren't completely unfounded. The levitating device had already made Catherine the center of attention in the lobby. No one was bold enough to outright stare at her, perhaps due to my presence, but the number of people glancing sideways in her direction numbered more than I could count on two hands.

"Oh, don't be a wet blanket, Emma. Not after Claire went through so much trouble to have this made for me."

"It would have been more appropriate if she had consulted me beforehand. I fear what might happen if the master hears you were given such a thing without his knowledge." Emma heaved a sigh, her brow creasing. I didn't quite appreciate how she seemed to care more about Clément's wishes than Catherine's, who she directly served.

"Your name was...Emma, correct?" I asked.

"That is correct, Miss Claire."

"Are you not Catherine's maid? Master Clément may be your employer, but is it not Catherine who you serve?" I asked, stopping in place. Lene's employer was my father, but I could trust her not to tattle on me if I acted up in particular ways. Her loyalty was sworn to me, as I thought Emma's should be to Catherine.

"It's fine, Claire. Don't worry about me," Catherine said.

"It is *not* fine," I insisted.

"I apologize if I've displeased you, but this is a matter concerning House Achard. Not even you, Lady *François*, have a right to interfere in our affairs," Emma said with a disapproving frown.

"Excuse me?" I couldn't believe my ears. "How dare you talk to me—"

"Emma, enough. That's an order. And, Claire, please leave it at that. I don't want to ruin such a wonderful day." Catherine smiled gently like she always did, but I could see she was genuinely pleading with me. She really didn't want to endanger the wonder of this moment.

"Catherine..." I still had much to say to Emma, but I couldn't allow myself to hurt my friend. So, I relented.

"Thank you, Claire."

"Let's go," I said after a pause. "They'll be starting soon." Still a bit heated, I began to walk off.

I couldn't understand how Catherine's own maid could fail to take her side. *Maybe if Emma were more like Lene, Catherine wouldn't have to be so alone.*

"There she is!"

"She's up, finally!"

Catherine and I were in our box seats, whispering excitedly as Loretta at last made her way onstage. The awkward mood Emma had cast over us had long since been cleared away by the musicians' performances.

Wearing an all-white dress, Loretta walked to center stage and bowed elegantly, then sat down at the piano and adjusted her seat height.

"She looks a little nervous," Catherine said.

"Understandably so. Her whole future hinges on this performance." It would all turn out perfectly if she earned an invitation to the Autumn Concert, but she would have to give up music for good if she couldn't. It would have been stranger if she weren't nervous.

You can do this, Loretta! I prayed in my heart for her success as she took a deep breath and began to play.

"This is *The Dead Maestro's Solo Exhibition*, isn't it?" I said, recognizing the piece.

"I believe so."

The composition Loretta had chosen for this recital was *The Dead Maestro's Solo Exhibition*, a masterpiece created by Metarlgesek, a famous composer from a country to the north. It was a grand composition with ten songs following its overture and interspersed with five interludes, and it was often arranged to be played by an orchestra, not just a piano. Its memorable melody and phantasmagoric tempo left a strong impression, but the skill required to play it was unlike any other.

And yet, somehow, Loretta's nervousness seemed to gradually ease as she played.

"She seems in her element," Catherine said.

"Indeed."

The look on Loretta's face was neither careless nor inattentive; it was rapture. She was caught in a trance, simply overjoyed at the chance to let music spring forth and frolic with her notes. Her hands danced over the keys and wove a melody that transcended sound into sight. I swore I could see the ten paintings Metarlgesek was said to have seen before composing this piece.

The critics present that day went on to describe Loretta as the pianist with a rainbow palette.

"She's amazing."

"Indeed, she is." Unwittingly, I had shed tears, for I knew I was seeing the fruits of Loretta's labors.

House Kugret was a military family, and because of that, unlike most noble ladies, Loretta had not initially been expected to marry into another house but to become Bauer's first female soldier. Such a thing had once been unimaginable, but the discovery of magic had changed things. Being successful early adopters of magic, House Kugret had been aiming to raise a female soldier for generations. That was why Loretta had been trained in martial arts from youth, and why she herself had previously never doubted that becoming a soldier was her raison d'etre.

Until she discovered the piano.

Loretta's father hadn't placed much focus on the arts in her upbringing, but she was still a noble. One day, around the time she entered elementary school, she was taken to a concert and became fascinated by the piano. But her wish to learn to play wasn't granted until she entered junior high. She was awful at first, compared to her peers, but she had improved quickly under the tutelage of Catherine's stepmother, and she was now one of our generation's top pianists.

After listening to Loretta's performance that day, I was confident that her journey wouldn't end there—and only a few days later, I was proven right when she received an invitation to the Autumn Concert.

"That was amazing..."

"Indeed..."

Catherine and I were still in a daze after leaving the auditorium, a credit to Loretta's immense skill.

"She really gave it her all."

"She has my respect."

One had to possess a great deal of talent to achieve such a level of performance. But I knew all the effort Loretta had put into her practice meant her success couldn't be attributed to talent alone.

"How about we share our impressions over tea, Catherine?"

"Oh, that sounds—"

"I cannot allow that." Emma interrupted. "The goal for today's outing has been met. Let us return to your room at once."

"Excuse me?" I said, angry that our happy moment had been dashed yet again. "What right have you to make that decision? Your job as a maid is simply to do as—"

"It's fine, Claire," Catherine said. "I was able to hear a wonderful performance today. That's enough for me. Thanks for expressing your frustrations on my behalf, but I'm all right."

"But—"

"You're going to see Loretta, right? I'll head back to the room first, then. Let's go, Emma."

"Yes, my lady. I bid you good day, Miss Claire."

"Catherine..." I could do nothing but watch as she swiftly left. Was I, a duke's daughter, unable to do anything to grant my close friend freedom? "...I won't give up."

No. I was Claire François, and I did not back down without a fight.

After finishing my shift at Cavalier, I went to the neighboring break room. I was exhausted, naturally. A lady of House François such as myself was ill-suited to such lowly service work. The princes seemed fine with it, so I didn't complain, but I considered such labor far beneath me and would never do it again if I had any say in the matter. All the same, being thought of as *unable* to do such work would have been even more infuriating, so I accomplished my assignments as perfectly as I could. Having to deal with the occasional thoughtless customer trying to make advances on me took its toll, however.

"Ugh..." I groaned upon entering the break room and seeing the commoner in the middle of changing clothes. I was about to turn on my heel and leave, hoping she wouldn't notice me, but no such luck.

"Are you on break too, Miss Claire?" she called.

"That's right," I sighed. "I still don't understand why I have to submit myself to such lowly tasks as serving customers." Thinking I might as well give up and stay at this point, I got to changing clothes and said the first thing that came to mind. My butler uniform had been tailored with practicality in mind, so I could take it off even without Lene's help. I was fully intent on changing myself, but the commoner was already almost done and so offered to help me. She could be of use at times, I supposed.

"You were really good at it, though. I was surprised."

"It's a given that I would know how to comport myself. Don't forget that I'm the daughter of the Minister of Finance." The commoner had endured a spot of trouble with some foreign royalty in the café a few moments ago. I'd stepped in to help because it had looked like it would bother the other customers and because she had been handling it so disastrously. There was no sense in dealing with those sorts head-on. You had to play modest and let them think they were your superior; that way, they'd dance in the palm of your hand. Such wiles were essential to navigating high society.

"Is that so? But I think I prefer how you normally are: so frank with your feelings, and sweet."

"What about me is *sweet*? Spare me the flattery. I'm perfectly aware I have a difficult personality." I knew myself well enough to be aware that sweet wasn't a word with which one could honestly describe me. Perhaps not many would have said so to my face, but I knew everyone saw me as a selfish noble girl. And it was true. I simply did what I liked. Someone who lived like that didn't deserve to be called *sweet*.

"You can certainly be thorny at times, but that's true for everyone to a degree."

"I wasn't trying to make myself sound special, if that's what you're finding fault with."

"Not at all. It just makes me sad to see you put yourself down."

"What do you mean? I'm not..." My voice trailed off as I thought back to my earlier words. I had indeed put myself down, and in a way almost begging for polite refutation. Such behavior was unbecoming of a member of House François. I sighed. "I must be tired from all this unfamiliar work. To think I would say such things to a commoner."

"I don't mind. In fact, I'm happy you did. I got to see your vulnerable side because of it. Might I be allowed to comfort you?" The commoner pretended not to notice my shame. She could be oddly perceptive at times. She never did anything that truly crossed a line and knew when to ease off. She furthermore maintained a firm distance between us, even better than I could possibly have maintained myself...

She could stand to be little less overbearing, though... Hmph. Fine. I suppose I could allow this commoner to accompany me on a whim.

I averted my gaze. "Don't be silly. Hurry up. I'll wait for you, so change already."

"Huh?"

"Why are you just standing there with that vacant look on your face? I'm telling you to come help me kill time."

She wore a look of utter disbelief. Goodness, what a face.

"Miss Claire?"

"Wh-what?"

"How do I look in this?"

I turned to look back at the commoner. She was wearing a butler uniform identical to the one I'd worn a moment ago, but the difference was night and day. I stuck out like a sore thumb in those clothes, but the commoner was the very image of the ideal butler. She looked...*good*. But I couldn't very well admit that, so I said, "I told you already. You look like a proper servant in those clothes, just as a commoner should."

"So you're saying I look good?"

"What's it matter?!"

I tried to avoid giving a direct answer, but she just wouldn't let up. Goodness. I puffed up my cheeks, indignant, when she offered her white-gloved hand to me and looked into my eyes. "If only for a short time," she said, "allow me to serve as your escort."

I admit that, in that moment, I thought she looked a little cool...

N-no, that's impossible! I couldn't have!

"Where shall we go?"

"Anywhere is fine, so long as it has nothing to do with food. Festival food will undoubtedly be unworthy of eating."

"Isn't food what a school festival is all about?"

"Perhaps, but I make it a rule not to eat anything of such low quality."

I traded small talk with the commoner as we walked down the academy corridor. The Foundation Day Festival was open to

I'M IN LOVE WITH THE VILLAINESS

commoners as well, so many could be seen walking about the academy. I wasn't too fond of the lower class, but tradition was tradition, so I begrudgingly overlooked their presence.

"How about here, then?"

"What's this?"

The commoner pointed to a classroom covered in eerie decorations. I had a bad feeling about this.

"It's a haunted house."

"Absolutely not!" I tried to run, but there was no escaping, as the commoner had grasped my hand. Only then did I realize that we were holding hands. *How could I have been so careless?!*

"Oh? Don't tell me you're afraid of ghosts?"

"O-of course not! I simply don't have time to waste on something as childish as—"

"Yes, yes, whatever you say. Excuse me, admission for two students, please." The commoner paid my complaints no mind and asked for admission. Now it was too late to wriggle out of this. "Miss Claire?"

"Wh-what?"

"Feel free to hold me if you get scared."

"Don't be silly—*eek!*" Something that looked like a zombie lurched out and startled me, causing me to cling to the commoner in fear.

I'll get you for this later, commoner!

"That was terrifying…"

"It let me see how adorable you can be, though!"

After leaving the haunted house, we came to a break area in the courtyard. I was dead tired after having the life scared out of me and didn't have the energy to admire the colorful spring flowers in bloom.

"Let's sit for a minute. I'll get us something to drink," she said.

"Don't get anything weird. I just want water, got it?"

"Your wish is my command." The commoner left, then returned after a few minutes holding two cups of fruit-infused water.

"You sure took your time."

"Sorry about that. Here's your water."

I scolded her even though it hadn't been that long of a wait. The commoner didn't seem to mind, however, and handed me a cup. I took a sip, relishing the water's faint trace of citrus, and felt refreshed.

"I also got this for you. Here."

"What's this...?" I took the item the commoner handed me, an intricate silver amulet with a magic stone set in its center. It was an item of Church manufacture—a good luck charm, meant for... "Luck in love?"

"I hope things go well with you and Thane," the commoner said with a smile.

I wasn't quite sure how to feel about this. "You really are strange."

"What makes you say that?"

"I know you only do it to tease me, but you've confessed your love to me before."

"And I mean it."

"Nonsense. If you did, why would you say you support my affections for another?" I toyed with the amulet's chain as I pressed the commoner for answers. I still didn't understand what she was after. She claimed to love me, yet she encouraged my love for Thane? It just didn't add up.

"I simply care more about your happiness than having my own love returned."

"How illogical."

"I can't fault you for thinking that, but it's how I truly feel," she said with a wry grin.

"Just why are you so taken with me...?" I'd thought it strange for a while now. The commoner had claimed to love me ever since we first met. At first I'd thought she only did it as some sort of strange flattery or joke, but becoming my maid would have been taking that too far. She had to have a real reason for all she did. Moreover, despite being so used to receiving the false affection of others, I couldn't detect whatever hidden motives underlay her behavior.

I would have been lying if I said I didn't put some hope in however she might answer. But she disappointed me.

"Because you saved me," she said.

Utter nonsense. How could it not be? We'd only just met on the first day of the New Year.

"You're teasing me again. I saved you? Ridiculous." I hid my disappointment and scoffed.

The commoner seemed crestfallen for a brief moment, but she recovered so quickly that I couldn't be sure I'd seen any sadness in her at all. "You can save me now if you'd like. Specifically with a hug or a kiss."

Yes, I couldn't have seen such a thing. She was the same as she ever was.

"Enough of your nonsense. Let's return. Our break's almost over."

"Yeees, ma'am," she droned and offered her hand. She clearly wanted me to take her hand again, but I wasn't so inclined.

"Your time playing gentleman is over. I am me, and you are you. I am a noble, and you are a commoner. Nothing more, nothing less."

"That's too bad. That means I've lost my excuse to hold your hand."

"You..." I sighed. The commoner only ever joked around, never letting me see her true self. How could I ever trust such a person? I walked off, leaving her to follow behind.

In the end, I never could quite bring myself to discard the amulet she gave me.

3

The Commoner Who Now Knows Her Place and Me

THAT NIGHT, I reflected on the day's events. The room was silent save for the sound of Catherine humming as she sucked on her licorice candy.

"Hey, Catherine?" I said.

"Yeees, Claire?" she replied with a sleepy drawl.

"What do you think of the Commoner Movement?"

I heard her shift in the bed above as she moved to hang over the edge and look at me, like she always did. "What brought on that question?"

"I saw some activists on academy grounds today and, well... I got a little irritated and lashed out at Lene because of it."

"Oh, I see..."

The Commoner Movement was an initiative seeking equality between nobility and commoners, despite the disparity in duty, history, and wealth that lay between us.

"Could you tell me more?" she asked.

"Of course."

I told her about the Commoner Movement activists we had spotted and how they'd called out to the commoner, only for Lambert to step in to break up our argument. I also told her of how Lene had made a remark in support of the movement and how I had scolded her for it.

"Hmm... Sounds complicated."

"There's nothing the least bit complicated about it. The notion of equality between nobles and commoners is simply preposterous."

Society would collapse if the two classes were made equal. Most commoners couldn't even read; giving them the same rights as nobles would only bring the country to a grinding halt. The idea was nothing more than delusional. That was why I had reflexively scolded Lene for sympathizing with such fools. I hadn't thought for a moment that she herself might support the Commoner Movement, but I supposed she was one of them in the end. Even if the premise was pure nonsense, the promise of a better life was doubtless a tempting one. And so I was worried. I worried she might one day come to actively support the movement.

"I see, I see. Well, have you ever thought about why commoners might want equality?" Catherine asked in her usual easygoing tone.

"Obviously they just want money. They envy our lifestyles without understanding the strict etiquette, customs, and duties we must adhere to."

It was true that the nobility were more affluent than commoners, and better educated as well. But there was good reason for that. When wartime came, the nobility were the ones who led soldiers into battle. In peacetime, they governed territories so the people could live well. Both duties required wisdom, sophistication, power, wealth, and military strength. Nobles were nobles because they had what was needed to lead—unlike commoners, who spent their days simply milling about.

"Mmm, you're probably not wrong, but I'm getting the impression you don't know much about commoners." Catherine cocked her head to the side—an impressive feat from upside down.

"Nonsense. I deal with them all the time; both my maids are of low birth. We even learn about their lives in class." One couldn't hope to govern without knowing how people lived, after all. Everything I'd been taught made clear that commoners were lazy, selfish, and overall irrational people.

"Mmm... I get the feeling that your understanding isn't very complete."

"How so?" I huffed. First Lene, and now Catherine was siding with the rabble?

"Well, for starters, the commoners around you aren't exactly ordinary."

"And why's that?"

"Lene comes from a super wealthy family, and Rae's a genius who got accepted to the academy. I find it hard to imagine that they're giving you examples of truly run-of-the-mill sorts."

"W-well..." I had to admit that Catherine had a point. Lene's family ran the Aurousseau Commercial Firm, which was a massive company that managed all of Bauer's magic stone mining. Their wealth surpassed that of even some lesser nobles.

That cheeky commoner was far from ordinary as well. She was a constant annoyance, yes, but she was also educated enough to have outperformed *me* in tests, was more familiar with etiquette than any commoner ought to be, and had world-class magical aptitude. They were certainly no standard to which to hold the rest.

"Besides, what you learn about commoners at the academy isn't the exact truth either, you know? We're getting those lessons from the people in power—the nobles who run the government and the upper-class commoners who work as their bureaucrats. They tell us what *they* think of commoners, so the story we're told is defined by the people holding all the cards."

According to Catherine, the ruling class assumed commoners were more slothful, greedy, and impulsive than they actually were because doing so better enabled them to predict and evaluate the worst possible outcomes. However, it could hardly be said that all commoners fit within the narrow bounds of those assumptions.

"Well, aren't you knowledgeable..." I said.

"Yeah, well, my mother's a commoner—and I lived as one for a while, so, y'know."

"Ah..."

Right. Despite being a descendant of House Achard, they treated Catherine coldly due to her mother's status as a mistress. On top of that, because her mother was a commoner, Catherine hadn't been born with noble status. For a time, Catherine had lived a difficult life as one of the masses, until the day Clément saw a use for her as a political tool and took her in.

"I'm sorry, Catherine. Have I unwittingly said anything that hurt you?"

"No, no, not at all. I've grown used to noble life, and I don't really care that I wasn't born into it."

"I see. That's a relief."

"But, well..." Catherine didn't finish her sentence, instead staring at me.

"Yes?"

"Weeell... I still think it'd be kinda cool if you tried to learn more about commoners, I guess."

"Why's that?"

"Your future husband's going to be in charge of the kingdom's finances, right? It'd be good to study up and become someone who can think for the sake of the people, just in case your future husband has a foolish idea and you need to rein him in." Catherine grinned.

"I'm already receiving education befitting the future wife of the Minister of Finance."

"Oh, I'm sure. But since you have the opportunity, you should try learning anyway. You won't regret it, I swear."

"Really now..." I wasn't too enthusiastic about the idea.

"Well, it's all up to you in the end. Just throwing my opinion out there."

"I understand. Sorry for bringing up such a strange topic out of nowhere."

"Nah, it's fine." Catherine pulled herself back up to her bed—then immediately hung back down. "Thought of something."

"Go ahead."

"What if you tried putting yourself in a commoner's shoes?"

"Huh?" I, Claire François, as a commoner? "Such a thing could never be."

"I know, I know; just hypothetically. Think of it as a thought exercise."

I paused. "I'll consider it."

"Great. Night-night."

"Good night, Catherine."

Catherine returned to her bed for good this time, leaving me to ponder her words. "If I...were a commoner?" But no matter how hard I tried, I couldn't envision it at all.

After meeting with the other Academy Knights to review the Commoner Movement issue and discussing the state of the government with Yu, I went to the cafeteria with Lene, Misha, and the commoner. Some girls called out to Yu, so he went to join them instead. Ever the popular prince.

Pulling me forward by the hand, the commoner walked with a blank face and an undoubtedly equally blank mind. The usual state of that fool. Lene wore a similarly blank expression, but her mind was surely abuzz with thoughts she simply didn't let show. Lene was nothing like that airhead.

"Heya, lassies. What can I get ya today?" one of the kitchen staff asked. As was clear from their accent, he wasn't a native citizen of Bauer but a refugee from the Nur Empire. He had apparently been a cook there as well but found himself unable to tolerate the place and fled to our kingdom. I could only imagine what tyrannical rule the empire's citizens had to endure.

"Get me the beef bowl!"

"I'll have that as well."

"The same."

The commoner, Lene, and Misha ordered the same meal. Beef bowls were a popular new menu item this year. They weren't quite to my taste, however.

"I'll have the beef stew," I said.

"Do you want bread or rice as your side?"

"Bread, please."

"Coming right up."

I'd have liked to eat something more refined, but I made do with what was available. After ordering, I moved to the line to wait for my meal. The meals here weren't cooked to order but premade and reheated, so I was handed my meal in no time at all. The four of us found seats and sat down.

We said, "Bon appétit," and began eating. The vegetables in my stew were a little soft—the meal having been premade—but that made the flavor of the stew seep into them a bit more, so it wasn't terrible.

"Rae, what do you think about that stuff from earlier?" Misha asked as she carried a spoonful of rice to her mouth.

"Hm? The what?" The commoner paused, confused.

"Are you referring to what we discussed with Yu, Lady Misha?" Lene asked for clarity.

"Yes, that. And there's no need to be so formal. We're both commoners, Lene," Misha said.

"But as a maid, it's only right that my speech remain proper. Please overlook it."

"I see... That's fine, then. But I'd like to ask what you think of what Yu said too."

"Oh. Well..." Lene placed her spoon down thoughtfully.

"Perhaps that was a bit too broad of a question," Misha said. "Can I ask you a different one instead?"

"Oh, yes, of course."

"Thanks. Then: Do you desire a noble lifestyle?" Misha asked as she scooped some red pickled ginger topping from her meal onto her spoon.

"Not really. Perhaps that's because I'm always taking care of Miss Claire, a high-ranking noble."

"I see... So you're familiar with the kind of life they lead. But don't you ever feel envious of the wealth discrepancy between you?"

"Well... I'm sure many would be, but my family is fairly affluent. Of course, we're not on Miss Claire's level, but we're up there."

"So you're somewhat similar to a noble already, despite being a commoner."

"Sort of. I haven't received the education or etiquette training that a true noble would, however." Lene took up her spoon again and resumed eating.

"What about you, Rae? Do you desire a noble lifestyle?" Misha asked.

"Nope."

"Why? Is it because you prefer taking care of Miss Claire?"

"No, I just want to live the life that suits me, and a life of luxury ain't it."

"Oh my," I said. "How surprisingly upright of you, commoner."

"Yippee! Praise me more, Miss Claire!"

"Don't get carried away now..." I already regretted saying anything. Ralaire looked at me expectantly, so I tore off some of my bread and fed it to her.

"Do you really mean that, though?" Misha asked the commoner.

"I do. For someone like me, academy food is luxury enough. The beef bowls I used to eat in my old world were way more—" She coughed. "Er, never mind, I've said my piece."

"Uh-huh..." Misha seemed deep in thought as she finally took a bite.

"Well, what about you, Misha?" I asked. "As former nobility, do you ever long to return to your old life?"

Misha didn't answer right away. Whether her hesitation was out of distaste for the strong flavor of red pickled ginger or simply due to her thought, I couldn't tell, but eventually she answered. "No, I suppose I don't miss my old life all that much."

"Oh? But you do a little bit?"

"I guess. It's more that I miss some particular parts of it."

"Like what?"

"I'm sorry, Miss Claire, but that's personal. I'm afraid I can't share."

"I see..."

I had an inkling that those parts Misha missed had to do with Yu. As the commoner had—rather inelegantly—put it before, Misha was likely still in love with him. Now that she was a commoner, her love would never bear fruit. But love wouldn't be love if it could so easily be forgotten.

"Returning to our earlier discussion, do you see anything to agree with in the Commoner Movement, Miss Claire?" Misha asked.

"Not a single thing. It's all pure nonsense," I declared. I had tried envisioning things as Catherine suggested, but my opinion remained unchanged.

"Then what do you think about the issue of commoner poverty?"

"If an individual is poor, they simply need to work. What's so hard to understand about that?"

"Well, not all work is equally available to all..." Misha said with a frown as she fed her red pickled ginger to Ralaire.

"Of course not. Not even nobles can freely choose to take up whatever line of work they'd like. One's birth, lineage, ability, and connections all play a role in determining who is most fit for a position. That's just the facts."

"I take it you don't believe in the equality the Commoner Movement preaches either?"

"Of course not. Equality is nothing more than an empty fantasy." I ate a mouthful of my stew. "Of course, the slimmer the wealth disparity, the better, but that's an issue for the proud statesmen of our kingdom to handle. Ideals have no place in reality."

"Miss Claire..."

"Yes, Lene?"

"Do you remember what Madam Melia told you?"

"Huh?" Had my mother ever said anything pertaining to the Commoner Movement? "About what?"

"About ideals and reality, Miss Claire."

"Ah..."

My mother's words came back to me then: *"Listen, Claire. A noble must not surrender to reality and abandon their ideals. If you are to call yourself a François, you must* stand by *your ideals and* make *them reality."*

She had said this to me long ago, back when she was still alive. When had I forgotten those words?

"And? What do you mean to say?" I asked Lene.

"No...it's nothing. Never mind." Lene cast her gaze down and finished the last of her beef bowl. "I'll return to your room to prepare things for bedtime. It's been a pleasure, Miss Misha. I'll see you two later, Miss Claire, Rae." Lene left to return the tableware.

I worried I had said something to upset her.

"It's all right, Miss Claire," the commoner said, filling her cheeks with food and continuing to talk—terrible table manners, really now. "Lene's not upset with you or anything. She's just hoping you'll do something."

"Huh? Like what?"

"Like that you'll change the way things are."

I hadn't a clue what the commoner was on about—which wasn't anything particularly new—but her words felt all the more important to understand now.

"What are you saying I'm supposed to do?" I pressed.

"That's for you to realize yourself. There's no point if I tell you."

"Haven't we had a similar exchange before...?"

"Have we?"

The commoner clearly wasn't keen on answering, so I had no choice but to let the topic go.

Just what did Lene hope I would do? What did the commoner mean by "changing the way things are"? What were "the way things are," anyway?

It wasn't until much, much later that I was at last able to truly grasp the issues Lene, Misha, and the commoner already understood that day.

Regarding Dole François
(MISHA JUR)

"**W**HY MUST I BE MADE to endure such a thing?" grumbled Claire, the young lady of House François. Her characteristic hair curls bounced as she walked, and she carried herself with an elegance that was readily apparent even through her childish pout.

By her side walked my best friend. "It's our job, Miss Claire."

"I am aware, commoner. But why must *I* of all people do something when anyone else would suffice?"

"Because we're the newest members of the Academy Knights. That of course means that the most basic chores get handed to us," Rae said in a teasing tone. I was a bit impressed that she could be so frank with Claire, all things considered.

We had been sent to the capital's market to do some shopping for the Academy Knights. Upbeat voices could be heard all around us as people conducted their trades along the bustling street.

"With a crowd this big, we might get separated. Shall we hold hands?" Rae offered.

"I'm fine," Claire said.

"You're fine with it? Then allow me!"

"In your dreams!"

"Aww..."

At a glance, you couldn't tell they were a commoner and a noble. I found myself a little envious and said, "Those two sure get along well."

"Don't they?" replied Lene, walking beside me with a smile. I intended to carry my fair share of our purchases but had a feeling she would wind up carrying the most. She was simply physically stronger than me. Stronger than Rae too, although that came as no surprise. As for Claire, well, it wasn't like we could make one of her status carry petty items, now could we?

"What are we buying, then?" Claire asked.

Rae answered, "Umm, ten sheets of parchment, twenty sheets of papyrus, two bottles of ink, one set of paints, one leather strap, one set of nails, and some tea and biscuits."

"So mostly office supplies."

"Most of the Academy Knights' duties are clerical work, after all."

Rae was right. Despite being called the Academy *Knights*, we were more like a student government. Our duties mostly consisted of paperwork, but I didn't really mind that. I thought it was nice to support everyone's pleasant school life through honest work. But it seemed that Claire didn't share that opinion.

"The biscuits are the only worthwhile thing on that list," Claire said.

"Indeed," I said with no real interest.

Perhaps recognizing the word "biscuits," Ralaire bounced joyously atop Rae's head.

"Let's buy the new sweets at Broumet to go with our tea."

"We can't, Miss Claire." I shook my head.

"Why?"

"Broumet is too expensive. If you want to shop there, you'll need to use your own money."

"How much did I bring today, Lene?"

"We didn't plan on private shopping, so only about ten thousand gold."

"That's not enough…"

Ten thousand gold was a staggering amount of money to a commoner like me, but it was nothing to someone like Claire. I felt all the more keenly aware of the wealth disparity between our classes. But I wouldn't have said I felt envious at that point.

"Let's just focus on work today," I said. "We can buy sweets next time."

"I suppose I have no choice," Claire said with a shrug. Then her eyes chanced upon something on the side of the road that made her frown. "Oh dear…"

I followed her gaze and saw two children dressed in rags and begging for alms. One had bandages around their legs.

"There have been more beggars since the conflict with the Nur Empire began," I said.

"Prices just keep rising…" Lene said.

The majority of beggars were women and children, as they were more easily able to garner sympathy. It was possible that the bandages on that child's leg didn't conceal a real injury but were rather a gimmick to elicit pity. Such craftiness was a must for a beggar, of course. A survival tactic.

"Prices might be rising, but aren't wages rising as well?" Claire said.

"Yes, but not fast enough. Employers tend to be conservative when raising wages, since it's difficult to lower them once they've gone up," Lene answered politely.

"Well, that's the employer's fault, then."

"The employers are commoners too, so they're not necessarily living comfortably either."

Claire stopped at that and frowned, thinking. Despite myself, her questions made me think she was far too ignorant about commoners. Or perhaps it was simply that she only knew what she had been taught and had never doubted the dim-witted image of commoners that the ruling class had painted for her. She might have been able to accept such false beliefs thus far, but one day, they would inevitably crumble around her—just as they had for House Jur.

A woman I didn't know called out to us. "Miss Claire?"

"Oh. Chief maid. What a coincidence."

It appeared the woman was the chief maid of House François and that I was the only one who didn't know her. Rae and Lene greeted her, and I, being a stranger, merely bowed my head.

"I'm here with the master on a shopping errand. He saw you and asked me to bring you to him."

"Is that so?"

I unconsciously straightened my posture. Claire's father was Dole François, said to be the sharpest and most able noble in all of Bauer. My father was a fan of his. I'd grown up hearing plenty of Dole's accomplishments and come to respect the man as well. And now he was nearby?

"Unfortunately, I'm working right now," Claire said.

"I thought as much, but he insisted."

"I see... Very well. Everyone, would you please accompany me?"

There was no way I could turn down an invitation to meet the man said to be the kingdom's greatest aristocrat.

We followed the chief maid out onto the main street. By the shoulder of the road was a single carriage of far superior make than the rest.

"Hello, my dear. And hello to your fellow students as well. Forgive me for greeting you from the carriage." A handsome man with blond hair resembling Claire's opened the carriage door. It was Dole, no doubt about it. I felt my hands go clammy from nerves. Rae seemed completely fine, but atop her head, Ralaire looked more still than usual.

"Hello, Father. Why have you called upon me? I'm busy with my work for the Academy Knights."

"Hmm? Do I need a reason to call my daughter over if I spy her in passing?"

"Father...I'm busy."

"I can't imagine you have any business that takes priority over me," he said, cocking his head to the side. Nobles often viewed themselves as the center of the universe, but my father had never suggested that Dole was such a man. How odd... "If you must go shopping, hop on. I'll even let these commoners ride with us, just this once."

"We aren't going to the noble district."

"That's all right. It's an aristocrat's duty to see how the other half lives every so often."

To think I'd be able to share a carriage with *the* Dole François! I was so nervous that my teeth were chattering, but I was nonetheless thankful for my luck.

The carriage, pulled by three horses, was spacious enough to comfortably fit all five of us and was a smooth ride all throughout. One could expect no less from the esteemed House François.

No one talked at first. Lene seemed awfully nervous, although I was of course no better off. Feeling awkward, I looked out the window and spied a group of commoners raising their voices.

"The nobles are exploiting us commoners!"

"They have no intention of helping our poor!"

"We have no choice but to take action!"

I figured they had to be part of the Commoner Movement. Curious, I gauged Claire and Dole's reactions. Claire scowled, displeased, and Dole simply looked as though he paid them no mind at all.

"How is the academy, Claire?" Dole said, breaking the silence. He smiled, pleased by the chance to speak with his daughter who now lived away from home.

"It's all right. The Commoner Movement is a bit annoying, but other than that, all is well," Claire curtly replied. Girls at her age found their fathers' inquiries meddlesome, I supposed, even if said father was Dole François.

"Ah, the Commoner Movement. A movement started by fools who failed to understand the intent of His Majesty's meritocratic policy. This is precisely why I opposed that policy from the start." Dole rubbed his temples and sighed. From what I'd heard, Dole stood at the helm of the noble faction opposed to the King's meritocratic agenda. It was natural that he would oppose the Commoner Movement as well, as it had been born from those meritocratic ambitions. "What do you think of it all, Rae Taylor?"

Claire's eyes went wide with surprise. "Father, what are you playing at? Not only do you remember the name of a commoner, but you actually address her by that name?" Even she, who knew Dole best, thought his actions were strange.

"I'm merely curious. I heard she has the best grades of any of the transfer students this year, and I would like to hear her thoughts," Dole said, as if to emphasize that his question had been mere whim.

"Yes, well..." Rae said. "Miss Claire asked me the same thing, but I don't care much for the movement. All I care about is being able to spend time with Miss Claire."

"I see. A good answer for a servant. But the fact remains that you are a commoner. Do you not yearn to live the life of a noble?"

"I'd rather see Miss Claire be happy than seek my own comfort. I don't long for the life of a noble. As long as I have enough to eat every day, I'm content."

"Is that truly how you feel?"

"It is."

Dole's blue eyes stared fixedly at Rae. If I had been thus scrutinized, I would have faltered and averted my eyes, but Rae fearlessly returned his gaze.

"Hmph. I see there are some commoners who still know their place, even in these times. I can only hope there'll be more like you to come."

"Much obliged," Rae said with a quick bow.

The sense of unease I had felt earlier only grew larger. Dole was...off. He was no different from the other nobles with whom I had grown so disappointed. The man my father had described was just, disciplined, and held compassion for the common man. He was supposed to be the embodiment of the ideal noble, but I couldn't detect so much as a shadow of that man in this carriage. Had time twisted him?

"Well, I must say I enjoy this company. Let's get something to eat, shall we? Chief maid, take us to Broumet."

"Yes, sir."

The carriage changed directions.

"Father, don't make such a decision on your own. I told you I'm here on business."

"It's just a small detour. If you have any problems, just give them my name."

"That's not the issue."

"Then what is it?"

Dole continued to act as though the world revolved around him, and I thought him more and more strange. I wanted to ask him: *Are you in fact the real Dole?*

"Have you had Broumet's desserts before? As a commoner, you've probably never enjoyed chocolate," he suddenly said to me.

I replied reflexively with, "I haven't."

Perhaps I was overthinking things, but it was almost as if he'd known I was about to speak and had been warning me not to.

"That's what I thought. This will be a novel treat, then. Broumet really does have the most innovative chefs in the game..."

Dole continued to happily chat away as we made our way to Broumet. He bought us some chocolates, after which we finished our shopping. The whole time, I observed him in the carriage and thought, *Master Dole... Just what changed you so?*

But my thought would go forever unvoiced.

Claire's POV

"WE HAVE A PROBLEM, Commander!"

"What's up?"

A knight barged into our Academy Knight meeting with a pale face.

"Moments ago, a noble student nearly killed a commoner student!"

"What?!"

The room was suddenly alive with action.

"Tell us what happened."

"Yes, sir. From what I understand, this afternoon, a noble by the name of Dede Murray got into a fight with a commoner boy in the courtyard."

"Dede did what?!" Yu exclaimed. Dede was his attendant; he'd been the dealer when we played cards with Misha and the commoner. "So that's why he hasn't been around..."

"Yu, let's let the man make his report," Thane said. "Continue."

"Thank you. It seems it started as a simple disagreement but grew more and more heated as the nearby students got involved." I could very easily see a small argument between a commoner and noble devolving into butting heads. The Commoner Movement had no doubt been a major influence. "Then...apparently one commoner made an insulting remark about Master Yu, and Dede lost his patience and attacked him with magic."

"That can't be... Dede would never," Yu said, in just as much disbelief as I was. No matter how rude someone might be, using power to make them submit was a last resort. I didn't know what the commoner had said about Yu, but I found it hard to believe it could have led to such violence.

"Perhaps the facts as reported are garbled and more will emerge in time. But this much is clear: The commoner was seriously injured and has been taken to the Church clinic, and Dede has presented himself to a military tribunal of his own accord."

Yu paled upon hearing that someone was seriously injured, but he seemed yet unwilling to believe that Dede could be capable of such a thing.

"Yu, go to military headquarters and find out Dede's side of things. That's fine, right, Commander?" Rod said, making a snap decision. It would be more helpful to accurately assess the facts first and make a decision only after that, rather than to act on general assumptions.

"Yes, please do. If he's in the middle of an interrogation, you likely won't be able to intervene, but he should be allowed visits from family or Master Yu in detainment afterward." Lorek nodded. "Given the circumstances, Lambert will escort you."

"Got it. Let's leave at once," Yu said before briskly departing with Lambert.

"We should try to find out the commoner's side of the story too," Rod said.

"Shall I go? They might be more willing to talk to me, as a commoner myself," Misha volunteered. While she looked collected as ever, she had to be all torn up inside. No matter how you sliced it, Yu was involved in how this had played out. It was clear she wanted to help him if she could.

"I can't allow you to go alone, Misha. Claire, go with her," Rod said.

"Understood."

"Then I'll go too," the commoner said.

"Thanks. Let's review the situation and act where necessary.

With any luck, we can nip this in the bud before it escalates." Rod looked everyone in the eyes. "All right, everyone, get to it!"

The clinics were medical institutions run by the Spiritual Church. The sick and injured could receive care at these clinics, but they weren't held in especially high esteem by the nobility. That was because the Church charged for their services on a sliding scale: The wealthier patients paid a higher fee, and the poorer patients paid a lower one. The Church was well liked by commoners for this system, which lent the Church a respect that exceeded simple religious faith.

There were various clinics in the city, but the one our injured student had been brought to was located on academy grounds.

"The patient is still undergoing treatment. Please wait a little longer."

We arrived at the clinic and explained our situation, but as the student was still receiving care, we had no choice but to wait.

"U-um...would you like some tea in the meantime?" A nun with red eyes brought us tea on a tray. I took a cup and thanked her. She then passed tea to Misha and the commoner as well. "Th-the treatment should be finished soon. P-please wait a little while longer." The nun bowed and left.

"That commoner probably said something outrageous... It's his own fault he got hurt," I said, having nothing else to do but talk while we waited. Nothing could justify the violence with which Dede had responded, but it was still the commoner's own fault for saying whatever it was he'd said.

"But isn't attacking him with magic a bit excessive?" Misha countered.

I agreed, but I couldn't bring myself to admit it. "A commoner shouldn't be mouthing off to a noble in the first place. Imagine if it were the other way around... When did commoners get so disrespectful?"

"So if the roles were reversed, it would be fine?" the commoner said.

Having been so used to her just nodding along with whatever I said, I was a little flustered. "Well...a noble shouldn't say anything untoward either, but..."

"But you're welcome to speak to me however you'd like. Please berate me all you want!"

"Watch yourself," I warned. It certainly wasn't the time for jokes.

"Miss Claire, we've finished treating the patient. You may see him now." After some time passed, we were allowed to meet with the injured student.

I gasped the moment I laid eyes on him. He was wrapped in bandages from head to toe. More of his body was covered than not. I hadn't expected his injuries to be so severe. Nothing he said could possibly have warranted such wounds. I thought back to Misha's words and found myself questioning who was truly in the right.

Misha and I were unsure of what to say, so instead the commoner was the one to speak first. She bent a knee at the base of the student's bed and met his eyes. "I'm Rae Taylor. What's your name?"

"Matt...Matt Monte."

"Hi, Matt. We're here on behalf of the Academy Knights to hear what happened to you. I know you must be in pain, but would you lend us a few minutes of your time?"

"No," he said sharply. "The Academy Knights are on the side of the aristocracy. I have nothing to say to you."

From what I understood, Matt was a protestor with the Commoner's Movement. He had a strong dislike of nobles that had only been exacerbated by this incident. It came as no surprise that he regarded us with hostility.

"The knights are on the side of the students," Misha said calmly.

"Spare me your official stance. Leave me alone." Matt looked away. He had no intention of discussing anything with us.

"Hey, Matt," the commoner said. "I didn't want to have to put it this way, but it would be better for you if you talked to us. Things are stacked high enough against commoners like you and me as it is."

"Damn right! There's no justice in this country! That's why we need to bring about—ow!"

The commoner's words seemed to strike a nerve with Matt. He tried to sit upright out of indignation, and Misha tried to calm him.

The commoner continued, "Matt, settle down. We're here precisely because we want to keep anything like this from happening again. Will you please talk to us?"

He looked away.

"Please."

I was surprised. The same commoner who always messed around was dealing with Matt so earnestly. Even though she and

REGARDING DOLE FRANÇOIS (MISHA JUR)

I were the same age, I couldn't help but think she looked more mature as she tried to warm Matt's stubborn heart.

Matt remained quiet for a few more moments before saying, "It was...it was just an argument at first."

Matt was the member of the Commoner Movement who had met with Yu. He had been seeking the aid of the Church through the prince but had been turned down. His fellow friends had comforted him, but he had become depressed about being unable to contribute to the cause. That was when Dede had warned him not to come near Yu again.

"You nobles are so full of it. You hoard all your wealth and power, and you don't spare a single thought for us commoners. And now we're not even allowed to petition for a better life?"

Matt had then criticized Dede, who initially responded with sound arguments but lost it once his master, Yu, was insulted.

"How could you be so ungrateful," Dede snapped, *"to the nobles who protect you?"*

"As we argued, a crowd started to form around us..."

A great debate—no, a shouting match between the nobles and the commoners began. Things escalated, until finally...

"I was so upset that...that the words just slipped out."

"You royals and nobles are nothing but parasites living off our tax money!"

"How *dare* you." I felt my blood boil. Had he no idea how much we nobles gave of ourselves, how much we sacrificed, to ensure the commoners could lead their lives?

The commoner stopped me before I could say anything more.

"Miss Claire, this isn't the time. I understand how you feel, but it's beside the point."

"But—"

"I will listen to your protests later. Right now, our job is to listen to Matt."

"Ergh..." I hated to admit it, but she was probably right. I looked to Misha beside me, and she shook her head as well. I relented and stood down, for the time being.

"And then? What did Dede do?" the commoner asked.

"He had looked upset the entire time, but it was like a switch was flipped when I said that. He pulled out his wand, and before I knew it, I was encased in a ball of flames." Matt hugged his shoulders and trembled, remembering the horror. "When I woke up, I was in this bed. It was only then that I realized what he'd done to me."

His voice was full of bitterness. Tears welled in his eyes. I felt my anger fade away as I looked on. "If the Academy Knights really are on the side of the students, then please, make sure he's punished."

"It's ultimately up to the academy to decide how to handle this. We have to hear out Dede's side of the story too. But we will do everything in our power to make sure you aren't silenced."

"I'm counting on you..." Matt said before sinking back into his bed.

"Let's let him rest. We got what we needed."

"Right."

I said nothing.

The three of us left the room behind. For a time, I continued to wonder just who was at fault here.

News of what had happened between Dede Murray and Matt Monte spread in the worst imaginable way. The event was dubbed the Courtyard Incident and was reported as a case of an arrogant noble victimizing a weak commoner, which earned the aristocracy scathing criticism from the populace.

It didn't end there. Tensions were already high with the Commoner Movement, and this incident only added fuel to the fire. The citizens, enraged, protested in front of the academy and the royal palace in swarms. The academy gates, usually left open, were for once shut tight. We nobles could do nothing but furrow our brows as angry shouts came from beyond the gate.

Pepi and Loretta let out grandiose sighs.

"None of that now, you two," I chided them. "That kind of sighing will only spoil the mood of our tea."

"I'm sorry, Miss Claire..."

"Sorry..."

We were at our usual arbor. Lectures were on hold for the time being, so the three of us had decided to have tea instead. Lene was with us to dispense her excellent service, and we had ordered chocolates from Broumet as our snack. Despite all that, the mood was dreary.

"I understand you're both worried, but let's try to enjoy the moment. The situation is entirely out of our hands," I said.

"That's...true, I suppose..." Pepi said with hesitation.

Loretta didn't reply at all.

The outrage of the commoners wasn't due to the Courtyard Incident itself but rather the verdict that had followed it. Despite the severe, life-threatening injuries Matt Monte had received, Dede Murray's punishment would be a short stint in prison—a mere week. Even I, with my bias toward my fellow nobles, could see this was unfair. The sentence was far too light. It was Rod's theory that the noble-elitist faction that heavily supported the status quo had pulled strings with the Church to orchestrate this outcome, although I doubted they had expected such blowback.

"Miss Claire?" Loretta placed her teacup down with a clouded expression.

"Yes, Loretta?" I said as gently as I could.

"I'm scared...of the commoners."

"And whyever would that be?"

"There's no telling what they might do once they get truly angry... Or what violence they'll resort to..."

"Such words aren't like you, Loretta. Are the Kugrets not a military house? Don't tell me the likes of commoners can scare you."

"It's precisely because I come from a military house that I know to be scared: The commoners outnumber us, and they have magic now. The kingdom's army may be stronger for the time being, but the moment the balance of power flips is fast approaching." Weakly, she added, "And this incident might be what pushes things over the edge."

"Aren't you overthinking this? Certainly the commoners are numerous, and yes, they have magic, but the army is trained. There's no way commoners could ever—"

"At best, a single soldier can fight three opponents," Loretta interrupted me, something she almost never did.

"Pardon...?"

"A single trained soldier is said to be able to fight no more than three enemies at once."

"Three? Only three?"

"Yes, and that's assuming neither side can use magic. Even the most well-trained soldiers soon meet their limits when it comes to close quarters combat."

I was surprised. I hadn't expected such a low ratio. Loretta's fears were grounded in a clear understanding of the difference in power between the aristocracy and those they ruled.

"But I'm confident I alone could easily face ten commoners, what with my magic," I said.

"That's because you're strong, Miss Claire. Some soldiers can use magic as well, but few of them are as powerful as you."

"I see..." I felt like Loretta was lightly scolding me for using myself as a basis, which humbled me a bit.

"I agree with Loretta, Miss Claire."

"Pepi..."

"I'm not strong like you two. I hate our practical combat classes with all my heart and couldn't move a single step when that water slime showed up. I just want to play my violin in peace," she mumbled. "Hey, Miss Claire? Is it not too late to change Dede's punishment?"

"What are you saying, Pepi? That's impossible," I replied. In the kingdom, it was generally understood that judicial matters were handled by the Spiritual Church. Nobles certainly had more than a little say in such things, but King l'Ausseil wouldn't approve of the nobility sticking their noses where they didn't belong.

"Perhaps for most it would be impossible, but maybe not for you, Miss Claire. Isn't there something you can do?"

"Don't be unreasonable. I'm as powerless in this situation as anyone."

"But you aren't. Can't you have Master Dole negotiate with the noble-elitist faction? I know he doesn't hold to their extreme beliefs, but he does still support the nobility. He has to have connections with them."

"That's..." That was actually correct, I realized. The problem was that the connection in question...

"Please, Miss Claire. Could you try to talk to Master Dole?"

"Pepi..."

"Let me ask this of you as well, Miss Claire. I don't want to have to fight the commoners."

I had no choice. I could never turn down a request from both of them. "All right. I'll try to talk to my father."

My friends smiled, slightly relieved.

"It would be pointless. My words would only fall on deaf ears." My father took a puff from his smoking pipe as he lounged in his leather chair.

We were in his study at the main François home. I had sent a letter requesting a visit with my father the day after I accepted Pepi and Loretta's plea. I had asked him to urge the noble-elitist faction to change Dede's punishment, but he had instantly shot down my proposal.

"Why? The situation as it stands is actively harming the nobility, and it's clear the noble-elitist faction are the ones who ensured Dede's punishment would be so light. Do they not feel any responsibility for the problem they've caused?"

"Those fools haven't the honor to feel responsibility. They only care about maintaining their status and gaining more power. I'm willing to bet they believe the commoners' anger will subside if left alone." My father took another puff of his pipe.

"But things cannot remain as they are," I said. "Even I can see the commoners are somewhat justified in their behavior. As things stand, their anger won't dissipate."

"Then what do you think we should do, Claire?"

"We need to sway the elitist faction, especially Marquess Achard." As I said that, I realized even I didn't believe this would be possible. At present, House François and House Achard were vying for influence over the first prince's faction. If we were to ask House Achard for a favor, they would almost certainly ask us to cede control of that faction to them in return. That was something we absolutely couldn't allow ourselves to do.

"I surmise from the look on your face that you've realized it's impossible." My father saw straight through me. I had no words to offer. "I'm sure we could make Clément agree to our demands, but the cost would be too great for House François to bear. Can you think of a reason our house should go so far for commoners, Claire?"

"I cannot... But—"

"Then we have nothing more to discuss. Stand down, Claire." My father swiveled his chair around and showed me his back.

I was powerless. So, so powerless. Stricken with grief, I moved to leave the room.

Then the faces of Pepi and Loretta surfaced in my mind. They had looked so worried as they asked me for help. Could I really go back and tell them I'd failed?

No. No, I could not.

Before I knew it, I had turned around. "If you can't do it, then I'll do it myself! Grant me leave to meet with Master Clément!"

A magisterial and aged door stood before me. Beyond it I would find Clément Achard.

After arguing with my father for permission to directly confront Clément, I went to the Achard manor. I was sure I would be turned away at the front gate, but to my surprise, I was granted an audience.

Lene was with me. The commoner had wanted to come as well, but Clément was a stickler for decorum, and with how poorly behaved the commoner could be, I had no choice but to order her to stay behind.

The hallway leading to this door was lavishly decorated and meticulously well kept. Everything about the manor was first-class. It was more than evident that Achard's lineage did indeed rival that of the royal family. Nevertheless, I couldn't let this shake me, or I'd never be able to hold my own in the coming negotiation. I relaxed the fist I hadn't even realized I was making, balled my hand again, and knocked on the door. The thick, imposing door resounded clearly with my knock.

"Come in," said a voice full of gravitas. My father used a similar tone from time to time. It was a tone unique to upper nobility, a tone to assert dominance.

"Pardon me." My knees felt weak, but I endured the pressure and politely entered the room.

Inside was a man a good number of years older than my father. He had thick facial hair and eyes that were a deep, dark brown. His hair was graying and neatly combed back, set with some hair product. He looked more like a reclusive hermit one saw in plays than the active political player he was supposed to be.

"You're Dole's girl... Claire, yes? What business could you possibly have with this old man?"

"It's a pleasure to meet you, Master Clément. But is it truly fair to call yourself an old man? I'm sure you have many years left to your name."

"Heh heh heh, there aren't many who'd dare shower me with such empty flattery. I see you truly are Dole's daughter."

"I have my mother's blood as well, and from what I've heard, she was quite the belle of high society."

"Ah, Melia. That's right. She was such a lovely rose, thorns and all."

We traded banter in place of pleasantries. I could sense the cautious probing barely hidden beneath his words.

"How old are you now, Claire?"

"Fifteen, Master Clément."

"I see... Oh, how time flies. It's hard to believe it's already been more than ten years since Melia passed. But I suppose the days just fly by once you're an old man."

"Indeed, time has flown by. But I still look up to my mother even now. And again, you are hardly as far on in years as you imply."

I could tell he was testing me by bringing up my mother, my sore spot. He wanted me to grow agitated and show disrespect, but I wouldn't fall for it. For the sake of negotiations, I could laugh this off.

"Hmm... Very well. You pass. Now state your business," he said.

"Thank you kindly, Master Clément." With pleasantries out of the way, the real battle began. "Would you be willing to reconsider Dede Murray's sentence?"

There would be no more beating about the bush from this point forward. I wasted no time in stating my aim. The roundabout approach had been on the table, but it would have been a foolish decision against someone as crafty as Clément. I had to fight him on the most even playing field I could, or I wouldn't stand a chance.

"What a strange thing to say. Judicial matters are handled by the Spiritual Church. Shouldn't you be asking one of their people for such a thing?"

I had expected this response. "Please, enough with the pretense. It is a well-known fact that your faction was involved in determining Dede's sentence."

"Hmm... All right, you have me there. So what is it you want me to do?"

"I want you to convince the Spiritual Church to revise Dede's sentence to one the commoners can accept."

Clément paused for a moment to mull this over. I began to worry what he could be considering when he opened his mouth and said, "What is it you seek to accomplish by doing this?"

"Excuse me?" I had no idea what he was trying to ask.

"You're a noble. Don't bother pretending you're so gracious as to pursue this change for the commoners' sake. What are you really after? Is it to drive a wedge between my faction and the Church?"

"O-of course not! I simply believe the current situation is unfavorable for both commoners and nobles alike!"

"Unbelievable. Then you were serious just now? I'm positively shocked. That's truly...hysterical." Clément chuckled quietly.

"There will be consequences for the nobility if the commoners are angered any further."

"Oh, how pitiable... Despite House François's great history, it's produced a lady who's genuinely foolish enough to worry for the commoners. Why, if the late Melia could see this, she would surely cry."

There was no getting through to Clément. He honestly didn't give a damn about the people.

"Master Clément, the times are changing. The commoners won't be content to live under our power forever. Unless we change as well, they shall supplant us!" I found myself surprised by my own words, for I hadn't even considered such an eventuality until now.

Marquess Achard shot a sharp glare at me and, as though having seen through me and my own shock, said, "Listen well, Claire. Times have changed many times throughout history, but the nobility have always ruled the common people. That is simply an ironclad truth of our world." He lifted a bell on his table and rang it. A servant quickly entered the room. "Our guest is leaving. Prepare a carriage."

"At once."

"Hold on! This conversation isn't over!" I panicked. I hadn't achieved a single thing. I hadn't even managed to explain how dire the situation was, much less reached the negotiation stage. If I didn't at least convince Clément to consider my argument, my entire visit would be for naught.

"We have nothing more to discuss. You've wasted my time... But perhaps I shouldn't be too surprised by the behavior of a girl who wastes time befriending broken things."

Fury shot through me. "Take that back! Catherine is perfect the way she is! What kind of father speaks of his own daughter that way?!"

"Daughter? Her? What kind of joke is that? Certainly she has my blood, but she has that putrid commoner swill in her as well. She's no daughter of mine."

"Why you—"

"Miss Claire, no!" Lene, who had been waiting quietly until now, rushed to stop me as I lurched toward Clément.

"Hmph. It would seem Dole and Melia suffered great misfortune when it came to their daughter. You only inherited Melia's thorns. How regrettable."

"You take that back! Do you realize who I—"

"Do *you* realize who *I* am?" Clément changed then, and the neutral air in the room grew suddenly oppressive. He projected an intensity that he hadn't possessed only moments before. "I am the twenty-eighth head of my house, Clément Achard. I've overlooked your transgressions to this point out of respect for House François, but I can make no further excuses."

I couldn't utter a word. As ashamed as I am to admit it, his intensity overwhelmed me completely. I'd met many nobles before, even royalty, even ones from other countries, but Clément was unlike any of them. He was a born ruler.

Lene pulled me away as she apologized with tears in her eyes, and together we left the Achard manor behind.

I failed to achieve a single thing and returned a failure.

"Don't worry. It's not your fault, Claire. It's all my father's." Catherine comforted me that night, but her words didn't reach me through my tears.

Taboo
(LAMBERT AUROUSSEAU)

"IS IT FINISHED?"

"It is," I replied.

We were in one of the Royal Academy's many research labs, specifically the one that focused on monsters. I was a member of this lab and worked there between attending classes as a student. Taxidermized monsters and chemicals used for work stood in various places around the room; my first sight of the lab had given me quite a scare.

The man I spoke with appeared to be a fellow researcher of mine, but he was in fact a disguised assassin who had been sent from the loathsome Nur Empire. I pointed at a small, hand-sized bell.

"Hmm?" he said. "That's the magic tool that can control monsters? It's smaller than I thought it'd be."

"That's because it was made for the army's use. It wouldn't be very practical if it were too big. As it is, it can only manipulate a limited type of monster."

"But it'll suit our needs fine, I trust?"

I hesitated. "It will." Soon I would use this bell to do the unthinkable—I would send a chimera to slaughter students of the academy.

"Is the chimera ready?"

"Yes, thanks to Master Salas." I thought back to the chimera incident a year ago, the very incident that had forced our then-commander Kristoff to resign from the Academy Knights. The whole thing had been orchestrated by Salas Lilium, chancellor of Bauer. His underlings had allowed the chimera to escape, and I'd reined it in with a magic tool—thus earning my place deep within the inner circles of the academy, just as planned.

For reasons unknown to me, Salas wanted to kill the children of powerful noble families attending the academy. Perhaps he wanted to end the lineage of his political enemies. Perhaps not. The aims of nobles were often lost on me. But whatever his reasons, the fact remained that I was a pawn in his schemes.

Before I knew what I was in for, I was in too deep. At first my only contact with Salas had been the mysterious man before me. He had promised the future my sister and I sought, and initially he'd only requested I help study the magic tool. If only I had known then what that would lead to.

I'd thought to back out, after which I was brought to meet Salas directly. He lent an attentive ear to the worries my sister and I shared, then explained how supporting his plan would help us. I became utterly convinced and agreed to support his ambitions—but wasn't there something strange about all that?

I paused in thought. What did our wish have to do with his scheme again? Something...something was off.

My doubts soon scattered like mist, however. *It doesn't matter,* I told myself despite my unease. *We just need to do as he says.*

"Looks like it's still working," the man before me said.

"Huh? Um, I'm sorry, what is?"

"Nothing, don't worry about it. Just thinking about how my father can be rather cruel at times. Not that I'm much better off."

"Er...?"

"Don't worry about it. Will you be ready to carry out the plan three days from now?"

"Yes."

"Good. I'll tell our men to make our move at that time. The rest is up to you."

"Um...Master Alter?"

The man's name was Alter, but that was, in all likelihood, an alias. He took on a different appearance every time we met and claimed to be a spy from the Nur Empire, but I couldn't even be certain of that.

"What?" he replied.

"Is all this...really okay?"

"What do you mean by 'okay'? If you mean for the nobles of Bauer, then of course it isn't. But for you two, everything will turn out just dandy."

I didn't reply.

"Don't get cold feet on me now. Isn't it your heart's desire to be wed to your dear sister?"

"Yes..." I loved Lene, who was my sister and thus the only girl in the world I wasn't meant to fall in love with. Our love was mutual, but at the same time, it wasn't meant to be. As siblings by blood, we could never truly be together.

But Alter—no, Salas had promised us a life where we *could* be united. So what choice did we have but to believe in that promise? What choices *did* we have...?

Alter stared at me. "It's wearing off. Bah, whatever. It only needs to hold for three more days, anyway."

"Huh?"

"Just talking to myself again. Hang in there a little longer, all right? Then you and your sister can officially tie the knot."

"Yes, sir."

"Good, good." Without another word, Alter left the lab.

I let out a long sigh. "Guess I'll head back."

I'd long since left my family home to live in the academy dorm. My reason for doing so was, of course...

"Lene, I'm back," I called out.

Lene was already out of her maid uniform and changed into her sleepwear. Officially, her room was in the servant dorm, but she visited my room to spend time with me practically every day.

My room was a bit unique in that it was meant for one person instead of the usual two. This wasn't because of any special accommodation or anything; I'd simply been assigned to a smaller corner room. Lucky me.

"The plan's a go," I said.

"I see... So it's finally time," Lene said sadly. I hadn't told her the whole scope of the plan. She would have opposed it if I did. "Are we really going through with this? It's just that it all...sounds too good to be true."

Lene was worried. My heart ached to hear her anxiety.

"It'll be okay, Lene. I can't tell you the details, but I've signed a contract with a trustworthy man who has the power to make our wish come true."

"But if he's so powerful, what's to stop him from ignoring that contract?"

I hesitated. I hadn't considered that. How could I not have considered that? I tried to reexamine my situation objectively. "...It'll be all right, Lene. Trust me."

"Brother..."

My head was too foggy to think clearly, but despite that, I was somehow certain things would turn out okay. Somehow.

"I see you made dinner for me. Thank you. But it's late, I think you should head back to your dorm," I said.

"But—"

"It'll be okay. Let me handle everything."

"I understand... Good night." Lene smiled weakly and left my room.

Now alone, I ate the food she had made for me. It was a simple meal, but I could tell it had been made with love.

I'd caused Lene nothing but worry for so long. But in a matter of days, that would be over, so long as everything went according to plan.

"Please bear with it just a little longer, Lene..."

Blithely unaware of my misconceptions, I looked forward to the happy days I still believed awaited us.

Claire's POV

*N*NGH...? *What's all this noise...?*

Through my dim consciousness, I could hear people talking.

"It's over now. Please give up, Master Lambert, Lene."

"Brother..."

Sensing something was off, I roused myself, but I feigned sleep for the time being. Someone was holding my shoulders, and something cold was pressed against my neck. I opened my eyes ever so slightly and saw two unfamiliar men on either side of me, a third nearby, and Lene and Lambert standing by the commoner.

What in the world is going on?

I tried to think back to the last thing I remembered. The commoner had asked me to remain in my room for some reason, and when I refused, she'd put me to sleep with her magic. So was she the cause of the current situation?

No, that was unlikely. The commoner wasn't someone I could blindly trust, but I just couldn't see her personality leading her to enact such a roundabout scheme. Then who had orchestrated all this?

"Hey, hey, we can't have this," one of the men said in a cheerful tone that didn't fit the mood. I couldn't quite see him from where I was, but I thought something was covering his face. Was he the ringleader?

"Without the magic bell, there's nothing we can do," Lambert said.

"Let me see it." The man took a bell from Lambert's dejected hands. If I recalled correctly, that bell was a magic tool that controlled monsters. Why was it broken, though? *"Return."*

To my surprise, the sides of the split bell rejoined as though time had been rewound. That was clearly magic, but I'd never seen anything like it.

"This should do it, yes?"

"Yeah..." Lambert replied, wide-eyed. He timidly took the bell and checked it, then made to ring it.

"Not so fast!" the commoner said.

"Don't move, Rae! Don't make them hurt Miss Claire!" Lene said sharply. I felt a sharp pain on my neck, at which point I understood that the cold object held against my throat was a knife.

The commoner made a face I'd never seen on her before, a mixture of anger and guilt. It was the face of someone angry, but at herself more than anything. Hmph. So it wasn't all sunshine and rainbows in her head after all.

My chest began to tighten as I processed what was happening. Lene had betrayed me. Lene, of all people—my dear Lene!

There had to be a reason. Her hand must've been forced somehow. But *why*?! *Why, why, why?!*

I trusted you! I believed you would always be there for me! And now you're leaving me too?

I was reminded of the hollowness I'd felt when my mother passed. The pain of the knife against my neck was nothing compared to the wound that still lingered deeper within me. Was I yet again helpless against a past doomed to repeat itself?

I gritted my teeth in defiance.

No. Things were different now. Lene was still alive, and I refused to just stand by and do nothing—for I was a noble, and Lene's one and only master.

"You genuinely believed you could handle everything yourself despite being a commoner? You must be even more conceited than I thought," I said to the commoner. I shook off the men holding me and cast my fire magic, enveloping them in flames. Three piercing shrieks rang out. "Even your screams are vulgar. It suits you, lowlifes."

"Miss Claire!"

"I don't quite get what's going on here, but am I right to think that the Aurousseaus are behind it?" I asked. The commoner looked dreadfully worried, so I stifled a yawn and smiled to show her that I was fine before I turned. "I'm disappointed in you, Lene."

Lene hung her head in shame.

I truly was disappointed in her. While I could never admit it, I had thought of her like my own sister... No, I supposed I still thought of her as a sister even in that moment. Her betrayal had been an unimaginable shock, but that couldn't stop me.

I only needed to think of how to stop *her*. I would take all my memories of Lene's happy smile, sunny voice, and gentle fingers running through my hair—and shut them away.

"Stick to the plan, you two." The same inexcusably cheery voice from earlier rang out as the flames were suddenly extinguished. One of the men stood up as though unharmed. He wore a black mask on his face, and he had to be quite strong to have taken the brunt of my magic and remain unscathed. "Do your jobs, and I'll help you escape abroad. Then you can change your names and live as lovers, not siblings."

So that's how it was. Forbidden love. I'd had an inkling that there was something going on between Lene and Lambert, but having it revealed like this was nonetheless a surprise.

It didn't matter. Not right now.

"Don't listen to him. Surrender," I said. I couldn't let their crimes pile any higher.

"I'm so sorry, Miss Claire," Lambert said sadly. "But it's too late for us now."

With that, he rang the bell.

The monster that appeared looked like the work of some terrible avant-garde artist. It was a haphazard amalgamation of a beast with the head of a lion, the body of a goat, the tail of a viper, and the wings of a bat. I recognized it right away. "Is that...a chimera?!"

Chimeras were monsters with durable bodies that could spew flame from their mouths. Most monsters were thought to be mutations of animals who ingested magic stones, but chimeras were a special exception, having been purposely created as familiars for military use.

"Claire, we have to run. Let's leave this to the army," the commoner whispered to me. That was the rational decision. There was no need for us to do anything—at least, that would have been the case under normal circumstances.

"No, I'll stop it here."

"Miss Claire?!"

"Every second we wait, it will wreak more havoc. And everything I let it get away with will be taken out on Lene."

"Miss Claire..." The commoner seemed taken aback by my words. She soon composed herself and sighed. "You're far too kind, Miss Claire."

"What do you mean?"

"Even after all that's happened, you're still looking out for someone who betrayed you."

"Y-you misunderstand," I said, embarrassed. It'd have been one thing if it were Lene, but how could this commoner understand me so well? ...No, I supposed now wasn't the time to ponder such things. "As Lene's master, it's up to me to take responsibility for her mista—"

"Yes, yes, I get it. You can be tsundere all you like, but we have a bit of an emergency on our hands and should probably focus."

"You can be real irritating, you know that? But you're right. Go call the army, I'll hold off the chimera."

"No way. I'm staying to fight too."

"I wish I could say I didn't need your help...but I think it's best I take your offer here." To be perfectly honest, I wasn't confident I could handle a chimera all on my own.

"Say, you consider yourself my master too, right?"

"Absolutely not. As far as I'm concerned, you're no maid of mine."

"Yeesh, you're still so tsundere!"

"Let me stop your fun right there, ladies." The man in the black mask interrupted our trivial banter, likely figuring out we were just buying time. "Lambert. Don't just stand there—get the chimera moving."

Lambert hesitated. "As you say." But at length he rang the bell and ordered the monster to attack me. "Go. Eradicate the nobles."

Following its master's orders, the chimera let out a vicious roar. It was the same stunning attack the water slime had used, Hateful Cry.

"Ngh, Miss Claire, can you move?" the commoner asked.

"Who do you think I am? I never make the same mistake twice." I had let my guard down the other day, but a Hateful Cry was no problem at all as long as one was mentally prepared for it.

"Are you familiar with the chimera's magic attributes?"

"Of course," I replied. The chimera had three attributes: fire, earth, and water. The lion's head could use fire, the goat body could use earth, and the viper tail could use water.

"I'll back you up, so go ahead and go all out with your attack."

"So I shall." I immediately pulled out my magic wand and created a spear of flame. "Burn to ashes!" I sent the spear straight at the chimera, but the beast simply swung its tail—with agility unthinkable for its size—and knocked it away. "It looks like straightforward attacks won't cut it. It isn't as stupid as it looks."

"Then how about this?" The commoner generated a stone arrow and fired it behind the chimera—at Lambert, who held the monster-controlling bell.

"Brother!" Lene cried.

"Not so fast." The masked man stepped in and blocked the attack with a wall of wind. "Aiming for the controller is smart, but you didn't even hesitate to shoot at a guy who used to be your friend. Have you no heart, girl?" he taunted.

I was sure the commoner hadn't intended to kill Lambert. She'd probably held back such that her attack would have incapacitated him. Even if he did get hurt, she could just heal him afterward with her water magic. We needed to stop him from using the bell, but that would be difficult with the masked man in the way. We were left with no choice but to fight the chimera.

The chimera opened its maw.

"Miss Claire!" The commoner leapt and pushed me down right before the spot where we had just stood was engulfed in flames. "That was a close one..."

"What was that?"

"The chimera's Fire Breath. It's more powerful than you can even imagine."

We were safe thanks to the water barrier the commoner had erected, but the same couldn't be said for the now ruined room. I was only just realizing that this place was one of the academy's research labs. The magic tools lying around were all burned to a crisp, and a section of the brick wall had melted.

"Let's take this outside," the commoner whispered.

"But it'll do even more damage there!"

"We'll lure it to the rear courtyard. The protestors are still mostly congregated near the athletic field. The academy students and staff are probably in the dorms."

"Fair enough." I nodded, then fired a flame bullet at the melted wall to open a space through which we could pass. "Run!" I yelled, purposefully letting our opponents know that our intent was to flee.

"Follow them. Don't let the noble girl slip away," the masked man ordered.

Lambert rang his bell and ordered the chimera to pursue us. The weakened building crumbled in our wake as we slipped out.

"Any chance they were crushed in the collapse?" the commoner asked.

"Doesn't seem like it."

With an earth-shaking rumble, the chimera burst out of the debris and approached at that same unimaginable speed.

I clicked my tongue and yelled, "Flame!" launching fiery arrows at the fast approaching beast. These flame arrows were smaller than my flame spears, but I could make more of them and maneuver them more dexterously. They made impact, but—"No effect?!"— the chimera barreled through the attack without stopping. I inflicted a number of small wounds, but they weren't anywhere close to enough. The beast neared and raised its wicked claws.

"Freeze." The commoner trapped the beast in an enormous block of ice. The chimera thudded against the ground, ice and all, its approach finally stopped.

"What is this utterly illogical magic?" I demanded.

"I'll muster up anything to save you, Miss Claire," the commoner joked. Even so, we weren't out of danger just yet. The lion head breathed fire and began to melt the ice away, freeing itself.

"Can't you freeze it to its core?"

"That would take too long, and I think the water attribute tail would remain unaffected."

"Then what can we do...?" The monster would only attack again. I could fight for a while longer yet, but the commoner was growing tired and would soon reach her limit.

"Miss Claire...for the first time in our lives, we must join hands and work together!"

"What do you need me to do?" Wasting time here would only endanger her. I urged her to continue, refusing to indulge her usual nonsense.

"Aim for its head. I'll use my water magic to boost your attack, like Master Thane did before."

"But won't the chimera just deflect the attack with its tail again?"

"Can you bring out that special move you used in the Academy Knights selection exam?"

"I can. But I have to gather my magic a bit to cast that."

"I'll buy us time. Get started."

"Are you saying I should trust you?"

"That'd be nice."

"Hmph. Fine then." I had no other choice. I would bet on the commoner's ability. "Flame!" I created a number of small magic bullets and fired them, then began focusing for Magic Ray. My bullets hit the beast's goat body, but it barreled forward, ignoring my attack. I remained still as the beast approached, a good distance between us yet. It opened its mouth, preparing for its Fire Breath attack, but I couldn't dodge without canceling my preparation for Magic Ray. *Commoner, show me my faith in you wasn't misplaced!*

"Freeze!" The commoner's magic was cast in time, freezing the chimera in its tracks. "Now, Miss Claire!"

The second the beast broke free of the ice, Magic Ray was finally ready to fire. The chimera's own flame came spewing out of its wide, gaping maw.

"Light!" I yelled.

Four rays of light tore through the chimera's flames, pierced its open mouth, and skewered its body. With a shriek, the chimera collapsed, this time for good.

"We did it..."

"Good job. I knew you had it in you, Miss Claire."

Relieved, the tension left us both all at once—leading to a moment of sheer inattentiveness.

"Impressive. But at the end of it all, you let down your guard, just like the naive child you are."

The masked man appeared out of nowhere and swung a knife down at me.

I saw the swift approach of the lethal knife and thought I was dead, but a strong arm swept in from out of nowhere and blocked the blow.

"Master Thane!"

"Seems I just made it." Thane's arm blocked the knife for me. Blood dripped from his wound, but Thane didn't so much as flinch.

"Well now, what do we have here? If it isn't the runt of the three princes," the masked man taunted.

Thane paid him no mind and swung with a magic-empowered fist. The masked man tried to dodge, but his mask was nicked, revealing part of his face. I couldn't make out much, but the gleam of a red eye amid darkness left an impression.

"Oh? I thought I had seen through that attack, but you're better than I thought."

"The army will be here soon. You should surrender."

There were plenty of talented magic users in the military, but Thane's proficiency in body-strengthening magic was in a league of its own. It was likely thanks to that skill that he had reached us first—not that I thought he should have. He was a prince, for crying out loud. What prince ran ahead while leaving his men behind?

"Is that right? Dearie me, I guess I'd better make a run for it." The masked man's cheerful tone was still as jarring as it had always been.

"You think you can escape?"

"Oh, I'll figure something out. I already got what I wanted anyhow."

"Hm...?"

"My initial goal was to kill as many nobles as possible, but... something even better has fallen right into my hands."

I was left wondering what he meant when—

"Ngh...?" Thane suddenly collapsed to a knee.

"Master Thane?!" I ran up to him, worried, only to see his pallid face.

"Poison?" he gasped out.

"Indeed, indeed. It's a special strain for which no antidote has been discovered. Please savor it," the masked man said gleefully before slipping away into the night.

A squad of soldiers arrived then, a step too late, and apprehended Lambert, Lene, and the other men. But I couldn't have cared less about any of that.

"Master Thane! Master Thane!" I clung to the now-fallen Thane and called out his name, but he didn't respond. His breathing was labored, his forehead was slick with sweat, and he occasionally let out pained moans. Ominous black spots formed on his skin. "Someone call a doctor! Call for a doctor now!"

"Miss Claire, please step away."

"But Master Thane's dying!" The thought of Thane dying had rendered me an absolute mess. The few moments we'd shared flashed through my mind. If I'd known it would end like this,

I'd have tried harder to get closer to him. But it was too late to think about what could've been.

The commoner's reply surprised me, however. "It's okay. I think I can neutralize the poison."

I didn't believe it was possible, but I reluctantly moved out of her way. With some preparation, she cast her water magic.

"The spots are disappearing!" I exclaimed. The splotches on Thane's skin gradually cleared away, and while he didn't rouse, his breathing eased. "Well done, commoner!"

"I'm just glad it worked."

In my joy, I hugged the commoner. For the first time ever, I felt genuinely glad that she was my maid.

"I suspected it was Nur Empire poison. Guess I was right."

"What?! Is that where that man was from?!"

The commoner nodded. The Nur Empire was a powerful nation to the east of our kingdom. They'd initiated territorial disputes with us numerous times.

"But just where did you learn of that poison...?"

"Mmm... I'm going to have to decline to answer that."

"What were you doing in the lab, anyway? It's like you knew Lene and her brother would betray us."

"I've been suspicious of Lambert for a while now. Lene really surprised me, though." The commoner's answer sounded reasonable at first, but it was all too convenient. I didn't want to believe it, but was it possible that she too was an imperial spy?

"Are you—" I began, but then Thane roused and opened his eyes. "Master Thane!"

"Claire... Is that you...? You're safe. Good."

"What are you saying?! Do you have any idea how much danger you were in? I thought you were done for..." I clung to Thane's chest and cried. *Thank goodness you're all right...*

Thane seemed unsure of what to do, but he eventually wrapped an arm around me and stroked my head. "I see I made you worry."

"I...I really thought you were going to die..."

"Sorry..."

"Umm, I hate to interrupt, but..." The commoner rudely stepped into the moment Thane and I were sharing. "Can we move? It's cold out here."

"Can you not read the mood?!" I must've made a horrifically angry face, but I was really just hiding the embarrassment I felt upon realizing how shameful my behavior had been. Truth be told, I was grateful that she was moving things along.

"It seems things are settled here." Rod appeared at that moment, alongside the rest of the Academy Knights. The field medic team carried Thane to the clinic for first aid. Rod fixed a stern look on the commoner and me. "So, what happened?"

"...And that's the gist of it."

We were gathered in the Academy Knight meeting room, listening to Rod explain the events that had transpired to everyone else.

The whole incident had resolved rather quickly. A number of protesting citizens affiliated with the Commoner Movement had stormed onto academy grounds, but once they learned there were traitors to the kingdom in their midst, the group had lost steam and dispersed. The Commoner Movement, which had gained momentum with the Courtyard Incident, entered a lull for the time being. The dissatisfaction the commoners felt toward the nobility hadn't faded, but they had the sense to know not to make waves after such a significant incident.

Claw marks could be seen here and there around campus, but the academy was, for the most part, peaceful once again. Craftsmen from the construction guild were still carrying in lumber and bricks for repair, but that would be finished soon enough, and by then, the whole affair would become nothing but a memory.

As an aside, chimeras were eventually deemed too impractical for military use, and further research was abandoned.

I stirred in my seat a bit as I listened to Rod speak. The space behind me and to the left felt terribly empty, for it was the place Lene had always stood.

Lene and Lambert had been arrested for treason. Though they had been coerced into their actions, they had still cooperated with a foreign power and been accessories in the attempted murder of nobles and royalty. Noble culprits might have been granted some leeway, but they were commoners. They were all but guaranteed the death penalty, even given the extenuating circumstances. Worst-case scenario, their whole family would end up put to death as well. The Aurousseau Commercial Firm had lost its standing overnight, and their magic stone mining and distribution rights had been seized. The only thing the family could do now was await the king's verdict.

"Will the Aurousseau family be...executed?" I asked. I already knew the answer, but I had to ask anyway.

"Most likely. They might've had their reasons, but their crime's just too serious to overlook."

"Right..."

A silence fell over the meeting. I wasn't the only one saddened here; the Academy Knights as a whole were devastated by Lambert's betrayal. A mere glance at Lorek was enough to make one want to cry. He had trusted Lambert like a brother.

"Oh yeah! Claire, Rae, I hear you two are going to be rewarded," Rod said cheerfully, trying to dispel the gloom.

"Huh...? Why?" I said.

"What do you mean 'why'? You guys identified the culprits and took down the chimera, right? Rae even saved a prince's life. It'd be weirder if you guys *weren't* rewarded."

"I expect you'll be summoned to the royal palace soon. His Majesty wants to grant you a reward in person," Yu added.

"We didn't really do anything deserving of a—mgh?!" I truly felt undeserving, but the commoner covered my mouth before I could say as much.

"Oh, is that so? We'd be delighted to accept," she said.

"Wha—commoner, what do you think you're doing?!"

"Relax, Miss Claire. I have a plan." The commoner leaned in and whispered her thoughts into my ear.

"I see... That's certainly worth trying."

"Right?"

The commoner's plan gave me a faint glimmer of hope in the darkness. It irritated me somewhat that she was the one who'd come up with the idea, but I was happy to go along with it regardless.

A few days later, we were summoned to the royal palace.

"And you managed to repeal the death penalty for them?"

"Yes, thanks to His Majesty and Master Thane's kindness."

The night after our audience with King l'Ausseil, I once again recounted the day's happenings to Catherine. Within the dark, there was only the sound of our voices and her sucking on candy.

"Catherine, you know you really shouldn't eat candy after brushing your teeth. That's how you get cavities."

"Oh yeaaah," she said with a sleepy drawl.

"Don't 'oh yeah' me. I checked your candy pot earlier, and you're already halfway through it!" Her pot was quite sizable too.

"But candy is just so yummy."

"Is that right..." I said with a sigh. I could tell it was pointless to try to talk sense into her, so I gave up and pulled my blanket higher.

"Putting that aside, are you really sure you don't want to...you know..." Before I even knew it, Catherine was hanging upside down from her bunk bed like always.

"What?"

"Are you sure you don't wanna see Lene off?"

"It's fine," I said after a pause, frowning. Lene might have had her reasons, but she and her brother had still committed treason. That I had been able to convince the king to spare her family was nothing short of a miracle. I'd done my part to help her and owed her nothing more.

"You know you want to, though."

"Oh, be quiet. I'm going to sleep."

"Running away from your problems, are we?"

"I swear you're starting to act more and more like that commoner..." Catherine had always been a bit like this, though; it just hadn't been so pronounced.

"You'll regret it if you don't go."

"I will not."

"You will too."

"On what basis?" I snapped, getting irritated.

Catherine flashed me a pained smile, something I'd never seen her do before. "Because to this day, you still regret your last parting."

She didn't say it outright, but I knew full well who she was referring to. My mother.

"That's..." I found myself without a good response.

"Do you really want to leave words unsaid a second time?" Catherine spoke softly, her gentleness slowly softening my stubborn heart.

I hesitated. "I can't. I'd never hear the end of it if the rest of the nobility found out I saw off a maid turned traitor..."

"Since when did you care what others think? It's not like you have a reputation to uphold. You know what people call you behind your back, right?"

The Villainess. I'd earned that moniker from the gossiping sorts.

"Keeping up appearances can't be that important, can it?" Catherine asked.

"Perhaps not for some, but I am an aristocrat."

"Mmm, that's fair. Even so, it's not the *most* important thing to you, is it?"

"That's..." I thought about it. Just how important was Lene to me? "Of course..."

"Yeees?"

"Of course I want to go see her!"

"Good, you're finally talking sense." Catherine smiled sweetly when I at last admitted the truth. "I'm sure Lene wants to see you too, but she's unsure if you'll come... No, I'm sure she knows you're in no position to come at all."

"Right..."

"And that's why you should go anyway. Because that's what's best for everyone," Catherine said with a beaming smile.

"But what would I even say to her..."

"What you say doesn't really matter. You can just say, 'You've served me well,' or 'Take care,' or something. Just don't skip seeing her off, okay?"

"Are such paltry parting words truly acceptable?"

"Absolutely." Catherine's certainty made me start to think she might be right. "You should take Rae with you if you're too scared to go alone."

"The commoner? Why?"

"She'll give you the push I'm sure you'll need. You tend to chicken out when it matters most."

"You're sure not holding back..." I was a little vexed to realize I agreed with her assessment of my personality. "...Do you think I'll be able to give her a proper farewell?"

"I'm sure you will. It's you and Lene we're talking about here, c'mon. As someone who's seen you two together firsthand, I guarantee things will turn out all right."

"A bold claim from someone who's hidden almost every time Lene's been present over the years..."

"Aha ha, you got me there." Catherine gave me a silly smile, and I found myself smiling a bit too. "Whether you laugh or cry tomorrow, what's most important is that you give her a proper farewell—for both your sakes."

"Awfully talkative, aren't you?" Catherine didn't normally speak this much.

Catherine looked surprised for a moment, which made me raise a brow, but she soon reverted to a smile. Perhaps it was nothing?

"Well, of course. My dear, dear Claire needs help; why wouldn't I get talkative?"

"Is that really why...?"

"Really-really. I'll even swear by the Spirit God if you want."

"You don't need to go that far."

"Pleaaase?"

"Why are *you* the one asking to pledge? How does that make sense?!"

"Eh heh heh."

Catherine was as difficult to fully comprehend as always, but for some reason, I genuinely believed that she was only doing the things she did out of care for me.

I said, "If I'm so dear to you, then why don't you come along with me to see Lene?"

"Nooo way."

"Why?"

"My father would never allow it. Maintaining appearances is all he's got, y'know?"

"You're really saying it all today, huh?"

"Am I wrong, though?"

"Perhaps not..." I thought back to my meeting with Clément. He certainly was vain about his reputation, but there was more to him than that. He was...the very manifestation of the wrongs of the noble world.

"Why the sudden long face, Claire?"

"Nothing, just thinking."

"Aha. I can guess what you're thinking about. It's best if you don't imagine your foes as bigger than they really are, though."

"I'll keep that in mind..."

Then Catherine gave me a serious look. "Back on topic, you're one hundred percent going to see Lene off, right?"

"Well..."

"Claire..." she said sternly.

"All right, all right, I'll go."

"Good. That's more like you."

"Goodness. There's no arguing with you, Catherine."

"Eh heh heh, you flatter me."

"I was *not* flattering you."

"Aw, figures." With a fit of laughter, Catherine pulled herself back up. I heard her getting comfortable in bed, so I did the same. "It might be a bit hard for you to see her off with a smile, though."

"Perhaps."

"But it'd be nice if you could."

"So it would..."

Several days later, I finally received notice of the day the Aurousseau family would be exiled.

On the day that the Aurousseau family was to be exiled, the commoner accompanied me to the border checkpoint connecting Bauer to the Alpes. It took us half a day to get there by carriage, meaning we had to take time off from classes to do it, but it was worth it if I could meet Lene as she passed through.

The majority of the Aurousseau family's assets had been seized, leaving them only the bare necessities as they moved to live with distant relatives in the Alpes. The Alpes was a nation that maintained long-standing friendly relations with Bauer, and their fertile land was famous for its agriculture. Their government was stable, and while it wasn't wealthy, the country was reasonably powerful. The people were relatively welcoming to both immigrants and refugees, making it the ideal country in which to find a new start.

However, while Bauer and the Alpes were neighbors, that didn't mean people could cross the border anytime they pleased. Our parting today would likely be for life.

In contrast to my melancholy, the sky above was blue from end to end. Feeling annoyed about that for no justifiable reason, I prodded my shadow with my parasol.

"The weather is nice," the commoner said.

"Yes, it is," I listlessly replied.

We watched the checkpoint from a distance for a while until the Aurousseau family finally appeared. The checkpoint itself was a towering structure built over the kingdom's largest highway. It featured a massive, sturdy gate that could be closed to fend off invading armies if needed. The Aurousseau family was being inspected there now; they had dealt in the magic stone trade during their time in the kingdom, but they wouldn't be allowed to spread the craft abroad—which was understandable, given that magic had strong ties to our armed forces.

Of course, while possessions and documents could be checked, there was nothing to be done about the knowledge in one's head. Nevertheless, I had serious doubts that anyone from the Aurousseau family could ever reenter the magic stone trade. The Alpecian government would never allow it, if they wanted to remain in the kingdom's good graces. The Aurousseau family would just have to make do in other industries.

"You think the Aurousseaus will be all right in the Alpes?" the commoner asked.

"I don't know, but I've heard the head of the family, Bartley, is a capable man. They might not be able to regain what they had in Bauer, but I'm sure they'll at least get by," I replied. But my mind was elsewhere.

"Things will be harder for Lene and Master Lambert, though."

"Indeed…"

Their forbidden love had nearly led to the death of their whole family, so it came as no surprise that the family had decided to disown them. They would be left to fend for themselves in this new country. Consequently, Lambert wouldn't inherit the family business, a hefty punishment indeed.

"Even so, they have to keep living. As long as one is alive, a way forward will present itself." My words weren't a truth of the world but more of a wish. *Please, somehow, please let them find their way.*

"Looks like the inspection is over," the commoner said.

Sure enough, the Aurousseau family was approaching the gate. I was shocked to see how few of them there were. With the majority of their servants let go, almost all of those present were of the main family. In total, the group didn't number more than twenty.

The commoner spotted Lene and Lambert among them and ran up to the iron fence. "Lene!"

Lene noticed her and came over. "Rae, what are you doing here? And Miss Claire too…"

"Miss Claire said she wanted to say goodbye," the commoner said.

"I said no such thing. You insisted on bringing me along, no matter what I did."

"Aha ha ha... It's been a while, but I'm relieved to see you two are the same as always," Lene said with a smile. It was a weak smile, but who could blame her for that?

A silence hung between us. Finding it unbearable, I forced myself to timidly ask something that had been bothering me for some time now. "Lene, do you resent me?"

"Nothing of the sort!" Lene said, flustered. "It was only fair that my family be punished. It's thanks to your intercession with His Majesty that we're even alive now."

"But I was the one who caught you." I didn't think what I had done was wrong. Presented with the same situation, I would have made the same exact decisions. But I was still directly responsible for the situation in which her family had landed. Maybe, just maybe, if I had listened to Lene's worries a little more closely, none of this would've happened at all.

"No. I'm grateful to you for putting a stop to our violence."

"My sister and I have finally come to our senses," Lambert added as he approached. "They say love makes monsters of us all, and we were certainly no exception. We wanted our forbidden love to be accepted so badly that we let someone take advantage of us. It's only now that we see the depths of our wrongdoing."

Lene nodded in agreement with his sad words. "Be careful, Rae," she said. "Don't let anyone use your feelings for Miss Claire against you."

"I won't," the commoner said.

"Lambert, Lene," one of the Aurousseaus called. "It's time. Let's go."

The time had come to part. I felt like I had to say something, but I just didn't know what. The commoner handed Lene something and said a few words while I was stuck dithering, which left me even further flustered. *I have to say something...anything!*

"Farewell, then. Thank you for everything, both of you," Lene said with a deep bow.

"Goodbye, Lene," the commoner said.

In the end, I couldn't say a thing.

Lene smiled sadly and walked away.

"Are you sure you don't want to say goodbye?" the commoner asked me.

There was so *much* I wanted to say to Lene. I wanted to tell her I was thankful for all she'd done for me, I wanted to reassure her that things would be okay, and so, so much more. But my thoughts were a jumbled mess, and the only words that leapt at me were: *Give me more time.*

But there was no more time.

That conversation with Catherine surfaced in my mind.

"It might be a bit hard for you to see her off with a smile, though."

"Perhaps."

"But it'd be nice if you could."

"So it would..."

Before I could even think about what I was doing, I yelled, "Lene!"

Lene turned around in surprise as her figure receded. I thought I saw something glimmer in the corner of her eyes.

"I won't say goodbye! We'll meet again someday! Until then, be well!"

Lene was already crossing through the gate by the time I managed to utter those last words. I don't know if they reached her, but I could have sworn I saw her smile. But maybe that was just wishful thinking on my part. Regardless, Lene and her family had passed out of reach.

"She's really gone..." the commoner said.

I wanted to snap back with something about that being so obvious it didn't warrant comment, but I couldn't open my mouth. I felt like if I tried to speak as I was, tears would fall.

"Miss Claire?"

"What?" Could she not see that it was taking all I had to hold myself together?

"Can I hug you?"

"Of course not. Come on, we're leaving." I managed some words and turned on my heel, then briskly walked away.

"No need to be so stubborn at times like this," I heard her mutter from behind.

Hmph. Say what you will.

"Misssss Claaaaaire!"

"Eek?! What are you doing?! Let go of me!"

"No! I'm not letting you go until *you* let go of what you're bottling up!"

"Stop talking nonsense!" I tried to shake free of her, which only made her squeeze tighter.

"It's okay to cry, you know?" she said.

"D-don't be stupid. Who'd cry over losing a maid?"

"I can't see your face from where I am right now."

"Like I said, I'm not going to cry!"

The commoner squeezed me even tighter. "I know you don't want her to leave."

She so plainly put my feelings into words. I began to tear up in earnest.

"This world really isn't fair, huh?" she went on. "We can't even freely love who we want to love."

I suspected she included herself in those words, but at that moment, I could only think of Lene.

"*My name is Lene Aurousseau. It is a pleasure to meet you.*"

"*Hmph. I don't care about your name. You'll just quit in a week like all the rest.*"

We had met so long ago.

"*Um, Miss Claire, I'm really fine with just a maid uniform...*"

"*Absolutely not. I refuse to accept that my maid doesn't own a single dress!*"

And had since shared so many days together.

"*Listen carefully, Lene. You are my... You are servant to the one and only Claire François. That makes you the most important commoner in the country. Take pride in that.*"

"*I, Lene Aurousseau, swear to become a servant worthy of Miss Claire.*"

"*Good. Give it your all!*"

We'd opened up to one another.

"I know you're hurting, but please, don't talk about dying. That would make the madam sadder than anything."

"My last words to Mother ended up being 'I hate you.' Now I can never say I'm sorry..."

Endured hardships.

"Lene, Lene! I met a prince!"

"That's wonderful. What's the name of this fated suitor?"

And experienced joys.

We'd walked all this distance together, but now our paths were diverging. But this wasn't goodbye forever, for I was certain our paths would cross again.

Having gathered myself a touch, I muttered at the girl behind me, "You really are cheeky for a commoner..."

"Maybe you should punish me for my cheek."

"No. You'd just consider that a reward, wouldn't you?"

The commoner mock gasped. "Are you perhaps starting to understand me? All that's left for us is to tie the knot!"

"As if!"

And with that, I was back to normal. The commoner moved to my side, happy to receive my sharp words.

"I hope we can meet her again one day," she whispered, taking a last look over her shoulder at the checkpoint.

"I'm sure we will," I said with conviction—and a little hope. No matter how far apart we were, anything was possible so long as we still lived under the same blue sky.

Afterword

Long time no see. I'm the author, Inori. Just in case any readers weren't aware, this book is a spin-off of *I'm in Love with the Villainess* (published by GL Bunko and Ichijinsha)* that retells the story from the perspective of Claire François, the heroine. If you haven't already, I highly recommend you read the main series before this spin-off.

With that out of the way, let's discuss the book itself. Did you enjoy it? I wanted to try exploring the thoughts of Claire the Villainess with this series, and oh my, what a villainess she was at this early point, what with her prejudices against commoners and barbed words toward Rae, our protagonist of the main series. But there's also a sweeter side to Claire, as seen with her childhood friend Catherine and her good friends Pepi and Loretta. Please look forward to seeing how she changes as the revolution that brings her and Rae closer approaches.

We had some new characters appear as well, didn't we? There was Catherine, Claire's ever mysterious roommate and childhood friend; Pepi and Loretta, previously known for their roles as

Entourage Member A and Entourage Member B; Loretta's fiancé, Kristoff, and his father, Clément Achard; and more. Their stories are an important element of this spin-off series, so please look forward to seeing more of them too.

The year I wrote this book, 2021, was a turbulent one for me. It started with the manga adaptation of *I'm in Love with the Villainess* getting fifth place on AnimeJapan's fourth yearly "Top Manga I Want to See Animated" poll, which was followed by the novels getting released in their eighth language, and then finally, the series was published in paper for the first time here in Japan by Ichijinsha. (For the longest time, the series had been digital only in Japanese.) Way back in the afterword of Volume 3 of *I'm in Love with the Villainess*, I mentioned I had upgraded my protein source from chicken breast to the occasional thigh meat. Well, I have some good news, everyone. Having now finished my final declaration tax report (which I've been working on alongside this afterword), I can now say that I am officially at a level of financial stability where I can eat thigh meat *regularly-ish*! Thank you, everyone, for making this possible. I'll do my best to make this spin-off enjoyable, so please continue to support me from here on out.

I'd like to end with some acknowledgments.

To my editor Nakamura at GL Bunko: Thank you for continuing to take care of the series. None of these books would have been possible if not for you. I'm sure I'll cause you some more grief yet, but I hope you'll continue to have me.

AFTERWORD

To Hanagata: Thank you for agreeing to do illustrations for the spin-off. Your illustrations were wonderful yet again. I know you're busy, but I hope to have you next time as well.

To my partner, Aki: We did it—*She's so Cheeky for a Commoner* got published! Let's go celebrate on release day again.

And lastly, to all who picked up this book: I offer you my deepest gratitude. Thank you so very much.

Let us meet again in Volume 2 of *She's so Cheeky for a Commoner*.

—INORI, FEBRUARY 12TH, 2022

Also published by Seven Seas in English!